The Shadow Territories

TL Hoffman

Dedication
For everyone who told me I could.

Beginning

We believe what we see.
Disregarding the things, we cannot.
But, when the lines blur,
It becomes difficult to navigate.
To create order among chaos.
To separate the good from the evil.
Light and Dark is a battle as old as time itself.
Stories are crafted around the wars they wage.
Ebbing and flowing with each epoch.
But what happens when Darkness wins?
And Shadows rule the earth...

Chapter 1
Florence

Something moves on the periphery of my vision. A black smudge. An orb.

Lazily, the black orb skitters out of sight. Out of time.

Vanished, riding the waves of a world not quite our own.

I wait a breath and then look back down at my book, worn at the edges and well loved. The dog-eared pages barely cling to the broken binding. The words blur, any amount of concentration impossible as I search the room for movement.

Surely, I hadn't seen it. If I had, there would be some evidence left. Some state of matter grounding my confusion.

Yet, there is nothing around me that is unfamiliar or out of its proper place. A ladder to the loft is tucked into the corner, leading into the secluded darkness. The workbench taking up most of the back wall is covered in empty sacks, parchment and dull quills. Book-keeping ledgers neatly line the bookshelf to my right. The hearth at the far end crackles with a small fire, and the door that leads into the alley is locked tight.

A small seating area in front of the fire is cozy and welcoming. Not a pillow or blanket askew.

Everything perfectly aligned.

Must be my imagination.

This is how most stories start. An unnatural phenomenon disrupting an otherwise natural habitat. Then, the hero gets sucked into a netherworld and must battle demons, both physical and mental.

Not this day.

This day is like any other day. Stress and emotion and boredom. Intense, never ending boredom. Blowing a few strands of hair out of my eyes, I try to make myself comfortable and fail.

Call me a dreamer, but I long for an otherworldly calling. Something to make me more than, make me special, in a way that does not cause pain or fear in others. Just like all those strong female leads I read about, seeking something of myself in their struggles.

Sighing, I pick up where I left off, losing myself in someone else's adventure.

Today has passed just like all the previous todays. I wake to an empty loft, overlooking a store full of goods no one seems to want. A routine that never changes and a loneliness that eats away at my heart.

I am alone in this small hamlet I call home. An outcast. Were it not for the miller and the baker, I would be utterly isolated. They, at least, treat me like a human being; everyone else fears me. Crossing themselves when they think I am not looking.

Little do they know, there is nothing special about me at all. An orphaned girl who reads to pass the time and restocks a haberdashery no one visits.

The passing of my parents hit the town hard, but it hit me harder. I lost the only two people who were familiar with the demons I battle and understood the struggles I face. They loved me for me and helped keep the night terrors at bay.

No one understood why I would scream at night. I barely understood it myself, for the dreams would melt away the moment my eyes opened.

The nightmares are gone now, lost with my parents.

They say I suffered a mental affliction-one that will never heal. The only affliction I suffer is the hatred they blindly throw my way.

There it is again!

The barely visible motion of nothing. Well, maybe not nothing. The air holds a chill that numbs my fingers, and my hands tremble. Overwhelming panic descends, and a familiar sense of dread knots my stomach.

I attempt to ground myself, taking stock of my surroundings and my person. I am alone in my shop, sitting in the back, chasing away boredom with tales of knights and bloodshed. There is a stool beneath me, connecting my body to the floor, the earth.

Squirming, I cannot shake this drowning sensation of eyes I cannot see, words I cannot hear. Of feeling like there is a life outside my own understanding.

Time slows. The dust motes floating through the sunshine filtering past the cracks in the shutters go still.

The bell above the shop door rings, forcing me back into the here and now. The tinkling chime scratches my eardrums in an off-key warning.

Heavy footfalls crossing the building's threshold match the staccato of my pulse, and the edges of my vision darken. I hold my breath in anticipation. Of what, I do not know.

Setting my book aside, I rise from my perch.

Sometimes you don't realize that a moment is about to change your life until it is already happening. You are already well on your way down the rabbit hole of fear and disillusionment before you know.

For me, this was that moment. The moment when I don't remember walking around the dirty partition between my dreams and reality. When I come face to face with a living nightmare.

The faint sounds of the dead and the dying float through the air. Eyes as red as sin stare at me from inside a darkened hood. My pulse thuds in my ears, and my palms slick with sweat, hands twitching for a weapon.

Standing in the middle of my shop is something I instinctively know is not of this world. The shape is vaguely human but larger than any mortal man. Dressed in pure black, the outline around its frame quivers. Shadows dance around the creature, whispering dark secrets that swirl around massive limbs. Long, skeletal fingers stretch toward me and the sound of grinding bones causes my teeth to clench.

"We are what you seek," whispers the nightmare, breath leaving its body in giant puffs. "Fear cannot be outrun."

And like the worst of gamblers, I take my chances and run. I am no stranger to this terror, the paralysis of indecision and bone-deep horror. Adrenaline has rewired my brain, I do not think, I act.

I am around the partition and out the back door before I can even process what I've seen. What I've done.

Where am I going?

What the hell was that?

And why did I assume my story would be like all the others?

An echo chases me out into the street. "Careful what you wish for."

Thankful I had the foresight to don boots this morning, I slide my way through the muck and ruin of the alley behind my shop, trying to get my brain to catch up to my legs.

"I am a rational, sane person. I am a rational, sane person," I chant to myself, legs and arms pumping, propelling me out into town. At least I thought I was until I barreled out of there like the town drunk with death on my heels. There was something not human standing in the middle of my haberdashery. Crimson eyes looked through the outer bits and straight into my soul. Worming their way through flesh, bone and sinew.

Glancing behind me, I see the empty mouth of the alley. No dark shadows with demon eyes or a hulking figure lurching after me. In fact, I don't see anyone, anywhere.

I am utterly alone in the middle of town. Spinning frantically in a circle, I try to locate another human being. It is the middle of the afternoon in spring. The town should be filled to the brim with people shopping and artisans hawking their wares. The smithy should be alive with banging and roaring fires. The baker and his four daughters should be selling the last of their cakes.

Everyone has disappeared. Carts and stalls left unattended, doors ajar and food lies half eaten on plates. Grimsfield has turned into a ghost town.

My breath comes rapidly, fogging in front of my face. Teetering on the edge of panic, I protectively cross my arms over my chest to fight off the chill that has followed me outside. This isn't right. Looking up at the sky, the sun hides behind low-hanging clouds and the fragrant spring air is stagnant. Stale like the scent of decaying roses. Even the colors have disappeared, and in their place are washed-out grays and molten shadow.

As I make one more futile turn, I see a mass congeal at the entrance of the alley. Cursing myself, I search for a place to hide.

I shouldn't have stopped. I should have kept running.

Checking the creature's proximity, I am frozen in place. Deep blue eyes find mine, leaving me motionless, until suddenly, I am propelled backwards. The force of a large fist strikes my chest with the subtlety of a battering ram. I land hard on my backside, jarring my spine as my teeth gnash together. Blinking, a shroud lifts, and the world comes crashing into focus.

Pulling in a deep lungful of air, I watch as villagers mill about the streets, sunlight warming my neck. My chest aches with unwanted pressure and I ignore the strange looks cast my way. I am seated in the middle of the lane, covered in dirt and sweat, looking as bewildered as I feel.

It seems life has resumed, and I am now blocking traffic. A man with a cart full of blooms shouts at me to move my arse, and I savor the sweet scent of spring flowers.

Climbing to my feet, I dust off my pale blue dress, and for the first time since my parents' death, I question the fragile grip I have on my sanity. The nightmares may no longer plague my sleep, but apparently, they have found me in the waking world. I had been released from their clutches, only to be smothered by a fate far worse.

I skirt around the cart full of tulips and a group of women who are openly mocking my appearance. I raise my chin and thicken my skin. Words cannot damage if you do not let them. My parents taught me to recognize my own self-worth.

The whole interlude feels like a dream as I wind my way to the front of the shop. The bell rings as I enter, a cheerful sound and not the wretched ringing I heard earlier. I glare at it and someone clears his throat from beside the counter. Startled, I snap my gaze to the visitor and I'm met with an accusatory stare from our town's tax collector.

Oh no. I forgot it was the 15th, and I'm always late with the taxes.

"Good afternoon Mr. Fletcher," I try to say as friendly as possible. Although I'm sure the smile I've just plastered on my face is much more a baring of teeth.

"Miss Stuart, how lovely of you to join me. In your parents' shop. That this town graciously allowed you to keep." His look is disproving and his demeanor hostile. To say we don't get along would be a gross understatement. The fact that I am consistently late with my payments, only fuels his ire.

"Just stepped out for some fresh air. You know how stifling it can get inside on a beautiful day such as this," I say, trying to regroup and not show how rattled I am. Going toe to toe with Mr. Fletcher after what may have been a psychotic break could very well push me over the precipice of rationality.

"Hmph, did that include a roll with the pigs?" He asks looking down his bulbous nose at me. Tossing me final appraising glare, he turns and slams his ledger down. "Time to pay the piper Miss Stuart, I've given you enough passes."

"I have it right here. Give me just a moment," I say as I slip around him to the partition separating the back of the shop from the front. I duck around it and pull up short. Atop the stool I recently vacated is my father's dagger protruding from what looks like a note. I am shocked into stillness. Who was here, and who could have known where the weapon was stashed?

"I don't have all day. Money to collect," Mr. Fletcher yells, tapping his pen on the counter. Clearly, he's used up all of his patience for the day.

Rushing to the workbench, I snatch up the coin purse. The ominous position of the dagger will have to wait.

Fingering the worn leather, I draw strength from the bag which was handmade by my mother. These coppers are the last of my inheritance. The last piece of anything my parents left me, except for this failing store. My eyes burn, and I suck in a deep breath. Mr. Fletcher will not see me weak, I will not give him the satisfaction. I have been resourceful my whole life, and I will not let this minor setback steal my dignity.

I walk back out front, head held high as if I'm not about to hand over everything I own. Notching my chin, I place the coin purse in Mr. Fletcher's outstretched palm where he tests its weight.

"Here you are, as promised."

"The full amount better be here this time," he grumbles, eyeing the purse dubiously.

"It is, it is" I reassure him. I need you off my back, I think to myself.

"Very well, Miss. Stuart. You are safe for another month," and with that, he sweeps out of the door without another word.

I sag against the counter and let the yawning emptiness consume me. What am I going to do? I have no coin and a store full of goods I cannot sell. The money I make from those who still dare do business with me is not enough to keep me afloat. The rest of the town gives me a wide berth, blaming me for the deaths of my parents. Rumor has it I was a burden to them, the night terrors becoming too much. I forced them to their untimely end, driving them mad. They are not wrong.

Not willing to get lost in a melancholy reverie, I remember the dagger and slowly peer around back. The sight of it fills me with dread. Someone was here and found the hidden blade, leaving for me to find. My sanity may be slipping, but this is proof I was not alone. And somehow, a world reflecting the worst of my dreams exists.

Heart in my throat, I approach the offending weapon and examine the jeweled hilt. The four unique stones set inside beautiful scrollwork, shimmer in the fading sunlight stabbing through the open back door. The blade is double edged and a dark silver. The craftmanship is breathtaking. Beautifully violent.

A quick scan of the parchment reveals only a single sentence written in bold script:

⬚Go nowhere. I will return at midnight.

Unnerved and slightly frightened, I yank the dagger out of the stool and flip the paper over. Nothing on the back and nothing more on the front.

My fear morphs into anger. I can handle the occasional prank, but this has a more sinister edge.

Young boys will sneak in to see who can last the longest in the rows of oddities, thinking I'm a witch who will curse them. The ladies in town would rather die than be caught associating with the town pariah. The windows have been broken a time or two and the trash will end up scattered throughout the alley. Mostly harmless damage. Nothing as threatening as the note I hold in my hand. But I refuse to let them drive me out, the shop is all I have left of my parents. It is my home and I have nowhere else to go.

I stick my head out the backdoor and check up and down the alley.

Whoever was here is long gone.

Chapter 2
Florence

The sun slowly descends below the tree line while I continue to debate the intelligence of being here.

I locked the door hours ago, too flustered to maintain the pretense of being open. Pacing past the rows of odds and ends, I can't get my mind to quiet as I catalogue and re-catalogue the inventory.

Dried spices, teas and sugars line the first few shelves, followed by knitting needles, yarn and fabric. Seeds and potatoes take up the space by the counter and I can smell the soaps and salves muddling together over by the window. My parents always sold a strange variety 0f useful goods and I tried to do the same.

After my third recount, I shuffle to the back and pick up the note to examine the lettering. Obviously in a hurry, the maker left deep indents in the paper I can feel with the pads of my fingers. The pilfered ink and quill were next to the coin purse I surrendered to Fletcher. Not a single drop misplaced in the haste of creating the message.

I must be daft if I am even considering staying here.

I let out a frustrated grunt and crumple the parchment, tossing it into the corner. I have always been a curious creature, and the mysterious note beckons me.

However, thinking on the events of a day, it may not be worth the risk.

A rap on the alley door draws my attention. Unwilling to take my chances, I peer through the bolt hole to see who it is. Standing in the alley is a face I know well.

Unlocking the door, I open it enough to peek outside.

"Samson, what a pleasant surprise," I say before swinging the door wide enough to let him through. Samson owns the mill on the edge of town and has been around since I can remember. He and my father grew up together. Short of stature with robust arms and a shock of white hair, he is one of the few friends I have left. Deep laugh lines and crow's feet accentuate his still handsome features.

Although he and my father were the same age, the death of my parents affected him deeply. The sadness and added responsibility of looking after me appear to have taken decades from him. I may be a grown woman, but I know he worries. Concentrating on my well-being was a welcome distraction, for both of us. He may look like he is sagging under the weight of time, but he is still as fit as a horse.

"Can I get you some tea?" I ask after I usher him inside, checking the alley for good measure. "I apologize for not having any prepared. I have been a bit distracted today." We always share at least one dinner together throughout the week and with the excitement earlier, I completely forgot it was today. I busy myself with the kettle, swinging it over the fire still burning in the hearth.

"No, no don't ya fuss. I admit I came ta see how ye were, lass. Gossip around town says ya bolted through tha streets like tha very Jackals of Hell were on yer tail. Took a nice tumble, and then walked back here like nothing doin'," he squints a smile at me. "What was all tha fuss, lass?"

I start to pace, not knowing how to explain my odd behavior but needing someone to speak to.

"Not one of my finer moments, I'll admit. What if I told you I thought a demon was standing in my shop this afternoon, would you believe me?" I ask, wringing my hands together. Once the words leave my mouth, I cannot take them back. Samson, humoring me, mulls this over, scratching his chin.

"Well, I've never known ya to be a liar, ma dear. Suppose there were a demon, what'd it look like?"

"I know this is going to sound nonsensical, but all I can recall is that it was a massive hooded figure with glowing red eyes." Shock registers on Samson's face, but he quickly schools his features.

"Do ya remember anything else about this creature?" He asks, rolling his hand in the air, urging me to recall any other detail.

"There was smoke, and the surrounding air seemed to get colder. I felt the worst sense of dread and panicked. That's when I took off and ended up in the middle of town," I say, explaining my odd behavior. "I came back to find Mr. Fletcher snooping around for his tax collection and that." I point to the crumbled note I've been contemplating all evening.

Samson gives me a weary look before snatching it off the ground, smoothing it out. Eyes going wide he looks up at me and whispers, "Where did ya get this?"

"It was on the stool with my father's dagger through it," I stammer, his intensity making me nervous. His flippant attitude is replaced by a commanding presence, and I realize just how intimidating short Samson can be. Something I've only witnessed once before, the day my parents died.

"Tell me everythin'," he demands. "Speak, child."

I hold up my hands defensively, recounting exactly what happened. "I was in the back when I felt a sense of foreboding. The bell above the door rang, and I walked around front to find a creature in dark robes taking up half of my shop, watching me with those eyes. I ran out the backdoor and found myself alone in the middle of town. The sun disappeared, and the air turned cold, numbing me to my bones. Everyone had vanished. There was half eaten food resting on plates and doors left wide open, but there was no one in sight."

"Shite. How did ya get back? How did ya get back to ta this side?" Samson seems almost crazed now, questions coming rapid fire. He stalks toward me, waving the parchment in the air.

"Another hooded figure appeared but it had blue eyes. I blinked, something knocked me in the chest, sending me flying and life restarted," I say as I sit heavily on the stool and eye Samson. He is now pacing, and a deep knot of fear settles in my stomach. It feels as if I've swallowed lead.

"What the devil is going on?" I ask Samson as he walks a circuit around my back room, note clenched in hand.

"Ya were visited by a Reaper child," he states, looking at me with worry, awe and a little fear. He resumes his back and forth, muttering to himself, "We have ta hide," he says, staring past me. "I promised them I would keep her safe, look after her. How'd he find her? They'll have me head."

"Wait, what are you talking about?" I demand, rising from the stool to step in his path. He halts, looking at me like he just remembered I was in the room. "You know what is happening? What that thing was?"

"Oh no, oh no I shouldna have said anythin' but we gotta move, now." Samson grabs a bag from my workbench and marches to the front. He starts collecting teas and herbs, rope and canvas, dried meats and a loaf of bread, stuffing them all into the sack. "Grab yer cloak and as many of your father's daggers as ye can find," he yells to me.

"But he only had the one," I say as confused as ever. "And why are we leaving? What is going on?"

"There should be at least one other lass, are ye sure it hasn't got a mate?" His question is muffled, and I round the corner as something shatters.

Groaning I grab a broom, looking for Samson's white head. He pops up by the medicinal herbs, muttering apologies. "Not that I know of," I huff, sweeping up broken glass, trying not to sneeze. "I don't make it a habit of playing with knives anymore. I only keep it close to help me remember them. But I need you to slow down for a moment, Samson. Why are we leaving?" I ask a little out of breath.

"I'll tell ye on the way. But right now, we need ta go ta ground." He meets my eyes and utters, "you've been found." At that final blow he shoves the pack in my hands, along with the blade and the note. Juggling the broom and supplies, I watch him dumbfounded. "Grab yer cloak and meet me at the mill. I'll have two horses saddled and word sent to Kalligan."

I'm left staring after him, listening as the door swings open and shut. I cannot sort through the thoughts crowding my head, the unanswered questions. The undeniable panic that filtered into Samson's eyes is now wriggling through my organs. Either I trust that he hasn't gone completely mad, or I stay and face the wrath of what is coming for me.

In this world where life has been unequivocally cruel, I haven't much left to lose.

It is full dark by the time I uproot my feet and hurry out the back door after Samson. I've decided to trust my instincts and listen to the only friend I have left.

I am not sure what Samson did before he came to Grimsfield, but he's been like family since his arrival. He was my father's childhood friend, and whenever I asked where he had been, he would get a faraway look in his eyes and say that he was just a traveler, an adventurer.

That was before he bought the mill.

He would come round after a long day to have an ale and share a story. He and my father would spin tales about growing up in the Highlands of Rolum. They always found themselves in some sort of trouble, weaseling their way out of punishment. Story time was always my favorite. It let me escape from here, at least for a little while. My mother would laugh and shake her head at their antics while I sat in her lap.

In those days I called them maither and aither, keeping to the traditions of Rolum. I don't know when I started thinking of them as mother and father. Maybe it was to distance myself from their memory. Masking the hurt.

Life had been so simple.

We lived in the loft above the back of the shop. Once I was old enough, I helped my mother run it by day while my father would aid Samson at the mill.

Before supper, aither would teach me how to defend myself. He wanted me to be strong. To be my own champion. He used to say everyone in the Highlands learned how to fight, even the women, and I never questioned it.

We would walk out to the hills beyond the center of town and train until we lost the light. The grasses would come up to my knees, but my father said it was good for training, helped build stamina. He would set up crude stick figures we would slice to pieces. Most of my favorite memories occurred on that hill. We escaped into ourselves and battled imaginary monsters.

My father was gifted with a blade. Each movement fluid and graceful, like he was dancing. He was impressive to behold. The dangerous tango was mesmerizing, and I could not help but try to be as good as him. I would practice all day, annoying maither when I should have been helping her.

Samson would sometimes watch our training, giving his input where he could, but he knew my father was the better swordsman. He would always say, "You've the best teacher lass, yer father was born with a blade in his hand." Aither would roll his eyes, but he never denied it.

After sparring, we would gather in the back of the haberdashery and break bread. We would often get invited to community bonfires and gatherings.

The townsfolk loved my parents, but always thought I was a strange child. I preferred swords over satin and lace. I asked too many questions. The other girls never wanted to play with me and the boys often left me behind. I would get teased for always having a soiled dress, but I loved to play outside. It never hurt to get your hands dirty, and there was so much to explore by the river.

But the worst was yet to come.

When I was ten, the night terrors started. I would wake the whole village with my bellows when one caught me in its clutches. Invisible demons held me under as I struggled to break free of the tormenting current. My breathing would become erratic and my screams would echo through the rafters.

Shortly after they began, the few children who would include me, stopped coming around. I was a leper. An oddity. Something to fear.

Try as they might, my parents could never wake me before the screeching started. When I finally came around, all I could ever remember was the suffocating panic and pain. I would scratch at my skin and claw at my face. I withdrew into myself and never came back out. I still bear the scars of my self-inflicted wounds.

I moved my pallet to the ground floor in case I got too close to the edge of the loft during one of my fits. Unsurprisingly, word spread that I was possessed by demons. My parents and Samson had none of it though, vehemently defending me, trying to explain the unexplainable. No one believed them.

As I got used to this new fate, I started to recognize one small detail that appeared in every episode. This little anomaly allowed me to pull myself out of the dream world. It always ended the same, I would spot a sliver of color out of the corner of my eye in an otherwise desolate plane. A glimmering beacon I would pry open with the tip of the blade I carried at my hip. Then I would awake at home.

I would look for other inconsistencies but could never remember anything else. This worked for a while, and I almost felt like a person again. I could wrench myself away from those unspeakable horrors easier and quicker than ever before.

But some things could not last.

My final act wrecked my small world, along with those in it. My eighteenth birthday was the last time I escaped from a nightmare, only to find myself living one.

That was five years ago.

I have not dreamt since.

I am almost to the mill when the back of my neck prickles; something is watching me. Quickening the pace, I jog the rest of the way, erupting through the door and slamming it shut behind me. It is dark inside, and I feel around for a flint and candle. A hand shoots out of the dark and covers my mouth. Another arm snakes out and pulls me away from the entrance.

"Shh lass, it is just me. Yer being followed," Samson hisses in my ear as we sneak through the lower level towards the back of the mill. Afraid to say anything, I shake my head against his hand before he lets me go. "Quickly now, there are horses saddled and waitin' in tha stable."

We creep out the back door only to be intercepted by a shadowed figure. Azure eyes blaze in my direction and Samson shoves me behind him. From under his cloak, he pulls out a sword bigger than I've ever seen and wields it with both hands. He rocks into a fighting stance and yells at me to run. The unknown hunter produces a blade of his own and charges at Samson who parries the blow.

I stagger and race away from the sounds of combat. The potent scent of straw, fresh oats and horses beckon me toward escape.

Behind me Samson yells, "Take the gray." Grunt. "She is the fastest." Steel rings off steel. "Get to the Keep in Darkwell on the coast and ask for Kalligan." That is the last thing I hear before I'm inside looking for the gray. She isn't hard to find, being one of only two horses in the stable, the other a black gelding. Restless from the sounds of the fight outside, she shies away from the stall door.

"It's all right, girl. It's all right," I speak in hushed tones to soothe the mare. Her eyes roll, and she huffs her agitation when I reach for her reins. I grab an apple from a nearby basket to coax her to me: which seems to do the trick. Carefully stroking her muzzle, I wish I knew her name. Samson yells and there is a heavy thud.

I am out of time.

Opening the stall door, I rush inside and swing myself atop the horse. Luckily, I am wearing thick leggings under my skirts, not that I can be worried about modesty at a time like this. I kick the mare's sides and we are out of the stable galloping past a pair of bewildered blue eyes. Turning the gray east, we head for the coast.

I am worried for Samson but dare not slow down. Glad that my pack has sturdy straps, I lean over the horse's neck and spur her on. Not wanting to be on the road, we weave through brush and branch. A stray limb hits my cheek and I barely register the sting of the cut.

Hooves sounds from behind; the chase is on.

Adrenaline pulses through my veins as my silent pursuer gains ground. A quick glance behind shows me he's closer than expected.

Urging the mare faster, sweat beads on my forehead. The dark stranger must have taken the gelding and is hot on our heels. But how is he gaining? He must be over two stone at least and Samson said the gray was the fastest. No time to contemplate the impossible physics as I maneuver the gray in and out of the trees. My skirts are torn, and my arms are covered in a pattern of welts from low-hanging branches.

It is no use; we are overrun.

The black figure has pulled alongside us and reaches for my reins. I try to turn away, but he is too quick. Grabbing hold, he pulls both horses to an abrupt halt in the middle of a clearing. Moonlight illuminates the glade and I still see nothing but hood, black clothing and blue eyes. I eye the horse and realize it isn't the smaller gelding. The stranger rides a top a massive Namidian horse, its black coat shimmering in the moonlight. The Namidian is the fastest breed in all the Three Kingdoms and is the currency of the Eastern realm.

Too terrified to move, I grip the reins until my knuckles turn white. My eyes are saucers and my dry throat protests any attempt to swallow. If this is how I meet my end, I will do it with my pride still intact. I will not go to my death with tears in my eyes. I will not shame my parents' legacy. Staring into the depths of the stranger's hood he utters two words,

"Stop. Running."

Chapter 3
Lucian

I tug on the girl's reins, halting her escape. Mouth falling open in shock, her haunted green eyes stare at me. The cut on her cheek glistens in the moonlight. I have an overwhelming urge to bandage it, but I remain as still as possible. I do not wish to startle her any more than I already have. She stills as a lamb would before a lion. I believe she may have stopped breathing altogether.

"Stop. Running." I say with an edge of annoyance. "You have nothing to fear from me, Florence."

At the mention of her name, she inhales a sharp breath, and her eyes flicker with confusion.

"How do you know my name?" She expels stubbornly.

"I know many things about you. For instance, you live above the shop you run. Your parents are dead, and I had to knock poor Samson unconscious, because I needed to stop you from running, and he was preventing me from doing so." Watching the shock register on her face is slightly amusing, but I did not have time to delay. Pieces are already in motion, and this girl may yet have an important role to play. Kalligan suspected she might be in danger and sent me to fetch her. However, he failed to mention that she might be hunted by Reapers as well. "You must come with me."

"I am not going anywhere with you!" She shouts, trying to jerk the reins out of my hands. Her frantic movements cause the gray mare to shy, almost tossing her sideways. Florence seems unaffected as she continues to yell at me. "Who, or what are you? And Samson had better still be alive."

"I promise, I only knocked him out," I reassure, trying to calm her agitated mount while maintain a hold on mine. "He will rouse soon enough. But he alone cannot prepare you nor protect you from what is coming. He cannot get you back from the Shadow Territories like I can."

She stills again, taking me in with her beautiful eyes. "Wait, you were there today weren't you? You somehow pushed me back into reality." Florence flutters her hand across her chest where the bolt of magic landed. I almost apologize but stop myself, she has no idea what she is up against.

"Yes, I am the one who forced you back across the threshold." Her posture relaxes, and I loosen the death grip I have on her horse. She is still on guard but seems willing enough to hear me out. "There is a lot you do not know. About who you are and who I think your parents were." Pausing for a moment I consider her companion.

A man I haven't seen in over a decade.

A man I was once close to. He took me under his wing and tried to tame the wild out of me. He was an arrogant son of a bitch, and sometimes I chaffed under his strict tutelage. We were both too stubborn but formed a bond despite my obstinance. Samson was, at one point in my life, the father I always wanted. He made me stronger, made me better, made me a fighter and gave me a purpose.

Seeing him today rocked me to the core, old memories bubbling to the surface.

He turned my cousin and I into the ideal warriors, and I will be forever grateful for this man. The skills he drove into me have save my life more times than I can count.

"We won't be leaving Samson behind. Let's go wake him, and we can travel to Kalligan's Keep together. I assume that is where you are headed based on the direction you were fleeing. Fortunately, that is also where I am going."

Her brow furrows, and I swear I've never seen a prettier pout. What a curious thought at a time like this. I catch a flash out of the corner of my eye and realize my mistake. Florence barely misses my neck with an unpracticed swing of a dagger.

I seize her wrist and easily pluck the knife from her grasp. Defiance and fear blaze out of her eyes. "I'll be taking that," I say wrapping the weapon in a cloth and tucking it into my cloak.

She glares at me for a tense moment and gathers her courage, "I do not know who you are, what you want or why you're after me, but I will not be going anywhere with you, sir. Give me back my father's dagger. Now." Haughtily she extends her hand and continues her stare down.

I admire her spirit.

My eyes briefly widen, realizing what I've confiscated, thankful I thought to wrap it in a cloth.

Recovering, I respond, "Not until I teach you how to properly handle a blade. Did William, I mean your father, not teach you anything?"

"He taught me enough," she huffs. "I'm just out of practice," she says with less confidence.

"Of course," I nod. "But I'm not giving it back." I watch her brow crease, amused further by her expressive face. Turning our horses around, I lead us back to where I left Samson in a crumpled heap. I feel a little guilty about how I man-handled him, but he refused to stand down. It's been ten years since he last saw me, and I was a boy then. I am no longer the lanky youth who spent more time pulling pranks than training. I've grown into my body and honed my abilities. He would be proud.

That long in the Shadow Territories really changes a person. Where there is no choice but to claw your way towards freedom, making decisions that leave their own scars.

I can feel Florence's curious gaze but say nothing.

Approaching a now moaning Samson, I send her a pointed look as I hand over the reins. "You've seen better days my friend," I direct Samson's way, swinging off my horse. Giving Javai's nose a pat, I walk over to help him up.

"Lucian is tha you?" Samson coughs as I help him to his feet. "I'd recognize that polished accent yer aunt beat into ya anywhere. What are ye doing here? I thought' ye were dead, lost to the Shadows." He gives me a once over and his eyes go wide. "It was you! Yer the one that jus' knocked me flat on me arse. These old bones don't move as well as they used ta," he says rubbing the back of his skull where I landed the blow.

"I am sorry, friend. I needed to get to Florence here before she got too far away." Removing my hood, I take in my old mentor's face. He is built like an ox even if he is short and a little rounder in the middle than I remember. Wrinkles cut craggy valleys through an otherwise handsome face, but I can tell he has seen better days. Roughed skin, wild white hair and eyes that have seen too much continue to take me in. Squeezing his shoulder, I smile down at him, "It's been a long time."

"It sure has me boy. Yer all grown up and definitely no' dead. I canna wait to hear what I'm sure is a thrilling tale," he jokes.

I let my hand and the subject drop, turning to look at the girl who is casting us both an odd look. She dismounts but does not come any closer.

"Allow me to formally introduce myself: My name is Lucian Campbell and I am a member of the Seraphim Order, much like Samson here and your parents before you," I say sweeping into a bow.

Straightening to my full height, her weary green eyes take me in as she remains quiet. After looking me up and down she raises a brow at Samson with a look that says: you know this person?

He sighs and looks at the ground, "I think it's time we had a little chat, lass."

"I don't believe this," Florence rolls her eyes and throws her hands in the air. "I thought we were leaving and now you're telling me we have to have a chat? And what, in the Three Kingdoms is a Seraphim Order?" Her eyes jump between us and I'm about to answer when she cuts me off. "You know what, never mind, maybe I don't want to know. I'll be in the mill when you boys decide to tell me what the plan is," without looking back, she stomps into the back of the mill and slams the door.

"She has no idea wha' is really out there, Lucian. We need ta tread lightly, but canna keep her in the dark anymore. She is somethin' special, and I'll no' have her spooked, ye hear me?" He dusts off his shirt, shooting me a warning glance.

"You mean to tell me that really is William's daughter, and you and he didn't tell her about your shared past?" I point toward the mill, disbelief coloring my words.

"Aye lad. You'll understand in time. Let's get this over with then, eh?" Samson leaves me in the moonlight and follows in Florence's wake.

Chapter 4
Florence

Striding past sacks of grain, I try to calm my nerves. The only light comes from a single candle I lit shortly after closing the door. The warm glow does little to settle my thoughts as the tiny flame throws long shadows along the walls and towering goods. It is full night now and I can't imagine we will be traveling until daybreak. The roads are treacherous under the cover of darkness, revealing all manner of danger. At least that is what I'm told. I've never left the safety of Grimsfield or the surrounding fields.

There isn't much else I can do but wait and worry the edges of my sleeves, trying to be patient.

My cheek feels tight, and I lift a hand to find dried blood and a shallow cut. During my ride through the woods, I remember a brief sting after coming too close to a tree.

One more scar to add to the others.

I wet the hem of my dress with spit and rub around the cut, trying to get rid of the excess grit, staining it red.

I can hear Samson and Lucian's muffled voices outside the back door and consider interrupting, my annoyance reaching its zenith. They must be deciding what I should and should not know. I really don't appreciate all this secrecy.

Taking a deep breath, I gather what little information I have. Based on what Lucian said, it would seem my parents led a double life. Or at least one prior to any memory I have. A life that was dangerous and exciting. The complete opposite of our life here. One they left behind so they could raise me in this humble town. I know nothing of this previous life. They never spoke of a place called the Shadow Territories or monsters with red eyes or boys who got lost in another world.

Another world.

I can't quite wrap my mind around it, yet I can no longer deny what I saw this afternoon. I felt it. Felt the unbearable cold and unrelenting pulse of fear. Saw a world that exists alongside our own, reflecting yet distorting it. Witnessed the power it took to get out of that mind-bending reality.

The back door opens and both men waltz inside, interrupting my musing. Samson wears a look of resignation and maybe a bit of shame. Lucian is unreadable. His gaze is unsettling. Now that his eyes are no longer hooded I can see they really are lovely, misty shade of blue, twinkling in the low light. Like the sky right before the dawn. I wonder if their glow was a trick of the light or I was just imagining the ethereal radiance. They both stop in front of me and glance at one another.

"Well," I prompt, impatient. "Are either of you going to tell me what, in the name of the Three Kingdoms, is going on?"

Samson crouches down to be eye level with me and begins, "Alright lass. Did ye ever overhear yer parents talk about a time before ye were born? Before they settled here in the Kingdom of Rolum?"

"No. All I know of the past are the stories you and my father would tell about the Highlands. No one ever discussed what happened in between then and now. I'm not even sure

I know where maither grew up." I say, tugging my sleeves over my hands.

Taking a seat next to me, Samson continues without looking in my direction. "Yer maither's past is complicated, and the Highlands were always the safest topic. Oh, how we missed the hills and the heather. The air is'na quite as fresh this far south. We'd get especially nostalgic after a wee bit of ale," he chuckles.

"Samson." Lucian all but growls.

"Right, right." He takes a break, settling in. "The important bits. Truth is lass, we - yer maither, aither and I - were a part of wha' is called the Seraphim Order. Lucian here too," Samson absently waves a hand in his direction.

"We are tasked with keeping Reapers, what ye saw earlier, and their menagerie of monsters, out of this world. They reside in a perverted version of this reality called tha Shadow Territories, more commonly referred to as tha Shadows. Everything ye think is a myth, Florence, is real. Reapers can cross in and out of this world at will through certain entry points, er gateways. The monsters, however, canna and require a Reaper to be their guide. Reapers are built of dark magic, magic that only exists in the Shadows.

"Their goal is to harvest and transport souls from this plane to the next. Fer centuries the Reapers jus' collected the souls of the dead or dying. There were, a'course, rogue Reapers that would attack the living. Yer parents and I would hunt them down and end their miserable existence. But then somethin' happened. It is no longer jus' tha rogues stealing tha souls of tha living and wreaking havoc with their creatures. It is all of 'em." He levels a weighted look at me.

"I am going to pretend that everything you just said makes sense, and that magic is real. So... my parents were essentially gatekeepers between this world and the next?"

"Magic is very real," Lucian grumbles. Samson shushes him, so he can continue.

"In a way, yes. Fer years we traveled around tha Three Kingdoms making sure tha Reapers stayed in check. Silencing rogues and carefully monitoring tha gateways. Eventually though, your maither became pregnant with ye. Will and Laila decided it best to become more sedentary and settled here, in the southern Kingdom of Rolum, where tha least Reaper activity had been seen. I continued to track the rogues fer awhile but decided retirement looked good on yer parents and followed suit. Tha rest ye know."

"So, what happened? When did the Reapers become more aggressive?" I ask, trying to keep up with this conversation.

"About five years ago." Samson falls silent and shares a look with Lucian, whose been staring holes in my head this whole time.

"Five years?" I ask. This is unbelievable, yet the information is starting to click events into place. "As in my parents died five years ago, and that was when the Reapers began stealing souls from the living in earnest." Still trying to process this, I ask a question I'm not sure I'm ready to hear the answer to: "Are you saying Reapers killed my parents?"

Lucian gives Samson an almost imperceptible nod before he continues. "Yes. Around five years ago we started gettin' reports that tha rogue Reapers were growing in number. We thought we would be safe here as tha closest gate is a couple days ride from here in Darkwell, under Kalligan's watchful eye. But we were wrong. Three rogue Reapers tha' traveled from the Darkwell gate showed up on yer eighteenth birthday, stronger and more powerful than we have e'er seen. Yer parents lost their lives fighting tha demons and their creatures. They took two of tha basterds with 'em though. Tha third escaped, and I assume made it back to tha Shadows. Word got ta Kalligan, and he shut tha gate permanently. It has been quiet ever since. I pledged ta Will and Laila I would look after ye should anything happen ta them."

"Is that why they were out on the old bridge? They were fighting off Reapers?" All I could remember of that night is waking up next to Samson, soaked and disoriented. A violent noise ripped through the air, and I watched the bridge collapse, the swift current carrying my parents down river. The search went on for days, but we never found the bodies.

"There had been so much rain..." I trail off as the familiar ache of their loss settles itself in my chest. I absently rub over the invisible hole they left.

"Aye lass," Samson's eyes soften. "Ye had walked out onto tha bridge and once they got ye back on land, instructed me ta get ye away from there as they engaged tha rogues. They felled two quickly but ye came to as tha third Reaper made it across tha bridge and vanished. Yer parents tried to follow, but they had done too much damage ta tha structure and it gave way," he says unable to look me in the eyes anymore. "That thing shoulda been demolished years ago," he adds, almost as an afterthought.

"And now this third rogue has returned to finish the job." It's not a question. I'm on the verge of hysteria. "But I've never even heard of Reapers or gates or your Order until today! Why has it come here after all this time?" I jump off the crate to pace my limbs full of nervous energy. This is madness.

Both men are looking at me expectantly and I have a wild thought that they are playing me. I've never known Samson to be anything but trustworthy, but this is all so foreign to me. My small world has been shattered all over again and is being put back together out of order.

"I dinna know," he says to his feet. Lucian's eyes still track my moments. Ever watchful in case I decide to bolt. "I had no idea one was even here until ye spoke of yer encounter earlier today. It is lucky Lucian arrived and was able ta bring ye back."

I look over at Lucian and ask the question that's been lodged in my throat, "How did you find me?"

"I can sense when something crosses in and out of the Shadows, like a ripple or vibration on the air. Although, I was surprised to find you there," he says quirking a brow. "By the time I arrived, the Reaper was already gone."

"That is rather vague," I shoot back, crossing my arms. I send a questioning look to Samson who has finally stopped studying the wood planks like they hold all the world's unanswered questions. "What do we do now?"

"I've already sent a message to Kalligan via Inna." Inna is Samson's Scarlet Raven. A species leftover from a time before the land was divided into the Three Kingdoms. Larger than a regular raven with wings that glow scarlet in the sunlight. These beautiful birds make great companions and messengers if you're lucky enough to encounter one. Samson found Inna injured in the northern Kingdom of Isiwen and nursed her back to health. She's been his loyal servant ever since. "So, he'll be expectin' us, but we shouldna move until daybreak. It's too dangerous on tha roads at night," he moves to stand. "I'll make sure tha horses are comfortable and we will bunk here tonight. There are spare blankets in tha closet there, I'll return shortly."

Samson leaves and I get to work creating makeshift cots, trying to ignore the man with the strange eyes.

"Go on ask me," he prods.

I glance at him over my shoulder, arms full of blankets. "Ask you what?"

"Why I look like the Reaper that was in the front of your shop this morning and how I was here at the right time. I know you're curious, I can tell by your air of mistrust." He waves his hand to encompass all of me.

"Oh, I'm that easy to read, am I? Ok then, Lucian," I spit out his name knowing full well he read me like a book. "Why do you look like the Reaper that invaded my shop this morning, and how is it you came to be in town as it happened?"

"For starters, your manners could use some work, a simple thank you goes a long way." The right side of his mouth lifts into a hint of a smile. I roll my eyes and he waits a beat before explaining. "However, Reapers are human in appearance. They are anything but, and the illusion makes them all the more terrifying. You probably noticed the eyes too. It is all you can see out of their hoods. That is what gives them away. I've spent the better part of the last decade trapped in the Shadows. In order to survive, I had to adopt their dress and demeanor. Coincidentally, I turned out to be as big a brute as they are," he puffs out his chest for emphasis and I try not to roll my eyes again. Anymore eye-rolling and they might get stuck that way. "As to why I was here to save the day, I've been tracking this Reaper's movement throughout Rolum. Somehow it keeps alluding me. Kalligan has his suspicions it is you the monster is after and he sent me to investigate."

Lucian sounds for all the world like he has done me the biggest favor when instead I am finding it difficult to remain calm.

"Great, this is doing nothing to comfort me," I grumble. "But wait, how is it you got trapped and seemed to have survived and found your way back?" I ask skeptically. I am still undecided on whether I can trust him, but he seems to be telling the truth. And if Samson knows him, he must be relatively safe.

"That is a story for another time. Just know that you can trust me Florence, I am on your side. There is something evil in the works here, I can feel it. The safety of the Three Kingdoms may hang in the balance, and somehow you're an important piece."

"Me?" I point to myself disbelieving.

"Yes," he says sternly, taking the load of blankets from me, stretching them out. "Your parents were two of the most famous hunters in the Seraphim Order before they settled down to live a quiet life with you," he looks up at me, intense gaze holding me hostage. "You were pulled in and out of the Shadow Territories with your soul still intact. That isn't something a regular girl can do."

"Then what does it all mean? What can I do? I can handle a blade, but I've never had to defend myself," I say, sounding frustrated.

"We can teach you," he says, reaching under his robes to hand me back my dagger. I unwrap it from the cloth and sheathe the blade, tucking it into my skirt pocket. "But for now, we need to rest and regroup with Kalligan. He may have more information about what is happening." He hands me a pillow and gestures to the pallet he made out of two blankets. "Let me find you some salve for that cut too, it looks angry."

I had forgotten all about it and suddenly feel very self-conscious. While his back is turned I try to rearrange my hair and rub at the dirt on my hands. He returns with a small pot that smells strongly of lavender. Dipping a finger into the ointment, he raises his hand to my cheek and I look away, afraid he will notice my blush. I've never been tended to by anyone other than my mother and I'm slightly embarrassed.

Warmth radiates from his touch and settles low in my abdomen.

Clearing his throat, he steps back, "There, all better."

"Thanks," I manage to squeak.

"The lavender should help calm your nerves too," he says. "Try to get some sleep."

The candle is nothing more than a stump, still weakly lighting the room. I can see a sliver of the moon through the window at the rear of the storeroom.

I guess he is right. I'm not sure I will be able to sleep with the weight of all this new information, but I need to at least try.

Samson returns, takes a blanket from Lucian and settles down beside me. "Get some rest lass. We've a hard couple days ride ahead of us, and we can answer more of yer questions on tha way. Kalligan will know what ta do." Patting my hand, he rolls over.

I nod to his back and turn to blow out the candle. Lucian is already there; our faces are inches apart. He really does have fascinating eyes and being this close to him, I notice he smells of fresh rain and sandalwood, a heady mix.

"It will be ok," he says gently and blows out the candle. "Goodnight."

"Goodnight," I whisper into the darkness.

Chapter 5
Florence

I blink my eyes rapidly but can't get them to focus. Shapes and colors weave in a kaleidoscope as I sit up and feel for the crate I know is next to me. I reach my hands out only to find empty air. I pull in a breath to cry for help but no sound escapes.

Panic. All-consuming panic.

It is as though there is a film over my eyes I cannot clear. I stumble to my feet looking for purchase and bump into a wall. Gliding my hands along the surface feeling the dips and grooves grounds me somewhat.

My eyes still refuse to cooperate, and I'm left disoriented and frantic. I try to rub away the blur as black spots dance in my vision.

The world comes crashing into focus.

I look at what I've run into and realize it is not, in fact, a wall. A mammoth of a creature stands before me heaving great breaths out of its hood.

A Reaper.

Backing away, red eyes swallow me whole. A thick mist envelops us both as screams filter through the air. Whirling on my heel I run, this scene all too familiar.

My cries for help are still nothing more than raspy pleas. The hunt has begun.

Flames dance along the perimeter of town, and I run for the wilderness. Prey fleeing from the predator. Weak in the face of my adversary. I come to a fork and take the left.

The rumble of a growl resonates off to my right. Tree limbs snap, and a black shadow crashes out of the dark depths. Teeth and claws flash in the firelight and I skid to a halt, changing directions. This new threat herding me back the way I came.

Putrid breath races across my back, and I know nothing but terror. The muscles in my legs protest, my silent screams echoing through my head.

Where is Samson? Where is Lucian?

Everything is ablaze. Flames dance across rooftops and reach toward the blackened sky. Soot and smoke claw at my esophagus, choking off any more futile attempts to call for aid. My eyes burn and the heat pulses against my skin, trailing sweat down my spine.

Before me, a crude platform materializes out of the smoke in the middle of the square. But this is not the square I know. I am somewhere else. The bakery isn't where it should be, and neither is the smithy. Atop the platform stands the Reaper pointing to something I cannot see.

I glance in the direction its spindle-like finger points and see a tower looming over the town. I can see the peaked roof and the thin archer windows, it must be attached to the outer wall. A violent snap at my heels keeps me moving.

Rounding the bend, I look up toward the tower and can just make out a shape swinging from the ramparts. A body.

As I get closer, I can see the man's eyes have been ripped out, blood tracking down his swollen face. His lifeless body swings by the neck, a rag doll left to rot. Slowly he sways in the night breeze and a soundless groan rips out of my throat.

I am mouthing the word help repeatedly hoping something, anything will hear me.

Unexpectedly, I hear my name on the wind. An intangible request, getting louder and louder. I do not risk slowing down but try to locate the direction of the sound.

I brave a look behind me, and there is nothing but void. The town is gone, replaced by a gray wasteland. My shoulder strikes something and I'm falling down, down, down. A black orb zips past me and I slam into the floor.

A vicious scream tears out of me and reverberates off the walls.

Familiar eyes hover above me, reflecting the fear I feel. I can't catch my breath and realize Lucian is shaking me by the shoulders.

"Florence," he sighs in relief. "You're ok, you're awake. You're awake." He helps me sit up and produces a glass of water from somewhere behind me. Samson is on my other side, white knuckling the blanket I must've kicked off.

"It was just a dream..." half a question, half an affirmation. I say it again out loud, more to convince myself than anyone else. I take a sip of the water to sooth my dry throat, the smell of smoke lingering in my nostrils. Was it a dream?

Outside the window, the sky is ablaze with the sunrise; mocking my uncertainty.

"I haven't had one since my parents died." Odd.

"What were ye running from lass?" Samson sets the blanket down, placing a reassuring hand on my shoulder. "Ye started moaning for help and kicked off yer blankets in such a rush ye startled us half ta death. It took some effort just ta wake ye."

"I was running and couldn't call for help. There was fire everywhere, and I saw a Reaper. It was there, shadowing me. One of its creatures chased me through a town I've never seen before. There was a man, hanging from the ramparts of a wall surrounding the city. He was dead, his eyes ripped out." I can't look at either man as the remnants of my dream start to slip away. The bone deep fear still sits heavily upon my shoulders.

I take a few shaky breaths and let the light from the rising sun chase away the last of the nightmare.

"What does it mean?" I ask once I can bear to look at Samson.

"I dinna know lass but it must have something ta do with the Reaper returning after all these years," Samson says, a hint of glee in his eyes and gets to his feet.

Lucian checks the window and looks at me with regret before speaking. "We need to be moving. Are you going to be ok?" He asks offering me a hand.

"Yeah," I say with more bravado than I feel. "After all, it was just a dream, right?"

Letting him help me to my feet I shiver at the contact. His hand is inviting as it closes over mine. A jolt of energy runs up my arm but is gone as quick as it registers.

His eyes briefly flash florescent blue before he looks away. I almost think I imagined it, but he looks guilty.

Letting me go, he quickly heads for the door. Over his shoulder he says, "I'm going to get the horses ready," before retreating outside.

Samson walks back over, and we roll up the blankets, preparing to make the two-day journey across Rolum.

The mill will be vacant for a few days and I follow Samson's instructions on closing windows and barrels. This takes a little longer than I expected, and we work together in silence. I'm too wrapped up in my thoughts, and Samson seems nervous. I've never remembered a dream this long after waking, and I can't shake the feeling that I'm still being watched.

My skin crawls with troubling awareness, and my hand still tingles where Lucian and I made contact. The nameless man's mutilated face swims through my mind, taunting me, those empty eye-sockets lingering.

We lock up the back door and find Lucian with the horses saddled, ready for our journey. As our ride begins, I'm convinced I'll see the swaying body all the way to Darkwell.

Chapter 6
Lucian

Grabbing our packs from beside the door, I leave Samson to tend to Florence. Her cries for help struck something inside me I don't want to examine too closely. I may always be haunted by the terror I saw in her eyes.

I know that look; I've seen it on my own face, staring back at me from reflective glass. When all hope is lost, you are forced to live within a dreamscape where there is always something lurking just out of reach. At least she can wake up from her own personal hell. I wasn't that lucky, and I carry the sins of my past around me like armor. I made a vow then, to never be weak again.

Saddling the horses is a welcome distraction.

I am just about finished when Samson and Florence emerge from the mill. Bruising from lack of sleep rings her eyes but she carries herself with courage, an admirable quality. If I hadn't witnessed the horrible episode myself, I could be convinced by her show. But I know she is battling her own demons. Brave girl.

"The horses are ready, we should set out, that way we can reach Wolfewater before nightfall," I say.

Wolfewater is the waypoint between Darkwell and Grimsfield. There isn't much there except inns and brothels, but it makes a good place to rest for those who don't wish to travel at night. Which these days is the smart choice. Being caught on the road after dark could mean death.

"Aye lad. We need ta get ta Kalligan's Keep as soon as we can." Samson agrees as we hoist ourselves up into our saddles and head east toward the coast.

The lane is only wide enough for one wagon to pass, and it is too early for much traffic. We have to move over for a few travelers from outside of town with goods to sell, greeting them as we pass, otherwise we ride in silence. Around mid-day we stop at a roadside inn to give the horses a break and grab a quick meal, saving our rations. We turn the horses over to a stable boy with instructions to water and feed them and head to find food of our own.

"We are making good time. Should be in Wolfewater by dinner," Samson observes.

The inn is small, yet well kept. Stairs by the door lead up to rooms that can be rented and a bar with a rather round gentleman tending it rests at the back of the room. He gives us a nod as we enter. The space is cozy. A door to the kitchen sits between the stairs and the bar, a fireplace with a small fire burning nestled in the far corner. Several tables are scattered throughout the space, all look rather worn, but clean. There is one other traveler seated at the bar drinking from a full mug, the hood of his green cloak pulled up to hide his face. I choose a booth at the back of the inn to keep eyes on all the exits. Samson grunts his approval, pulling up a chair next to my right. Florence sits across from me, shoulders slumped.

A young woman brings over three tankards of ale and asks if we would like something to eat.

"Yes, three bowls of stew please." I say, as a way of dismissing her. I wait until she returns to the kitchen before I lean over to Florence, "You've been silent as the grave. Is the dream still bothering you?"

"I am just trying to take everything in. Process. Also, trying to work out why the dreams have started again." She answers, grabbing her ale with both hands to take a deep pull.

I keep my voice low, regardless of the somewhat privacy we have, "The shock of the past day may have something to do with it. I'm sure all the talk of your parents and your past may have triggered something you buried deep. Not to mention you've also encountered your first Reaper. I remember the first time I saw one, I'm happy I didn't piss myself."

Samson snorts into his tankard but remains silent, eyes on the man by the bar.

"You're probably right," she says nervously, fingering the handle of her mug. "I do have a question for you, though, did you leave the note I found on my stool yesterday?" Taking another sip of her ale, her green eyes watch me over the rim of the mug.

The question takes me by surprise.

"What note?" I ask genuinely confused. Samson is still quiet, eyes returning to us.

She pulls a piece of parchment from the pocket in her skirt and gives it to me.

"You didn't leave this cryptic note stabbed through with my father's dagger? I saw you in the alley behind the shop before you brought me back, and I assumed you wrote it before rescuing me. Although, how you knew where the dagger was is beyond me."

I read over the eight words and swallow down my apprehension. This note worries me. The words are ominous and dangerous. Whoever wrote this could be following us, even now.

"Florence, I did not write this." I look up at her and she stills.

"Excuse me?"

"I didn't write this, and I don't know who did." I hand the paper to Samson who just passes it back to Florence. He either doesn't care or has already seen it. The serving girl arrives then with our food as Florence refolds the note and places it back in her pocket.

"Anythin' else I can be gettin' ya?" The young woman asks. She must be a relation to the barkeep, they have a similar disposition.

"No, we are fine, thank you," I hand her a few coppers and she moves to talk with the man behind the bar. Once she is distracted by conversation, I ask Florence to explain the dagger.

"I found it pierced through the middle of the note on my stool. I keep it in the bottom right drawer of the bench in the back, hidden under a removable panel. My father always told me to keep it a secret unless I really needed to use it. We have other weapons scattered around, so I left it where it was, forgetting it. I thought it was just something he picked up during his travels with you, Samson, and that he didn't want me to lose it. It really is a remarkable blade," her eyes take on a faraway look before she gets excited, "would you like to see it?"

"Nay lass, no' here," Samson stays her hand and looks over at the man he's been watching, drink relatively untouched. "Wait until we are outside." She nods and goes back to picking at her stew.

"I feel sick knowing someone knew where to find it." She alights on an idea, "it's connected to my parents' past, isn't it?"

"Aye, that's no' just any weapon," he answers. "It and others like it were created specifically by tha Seraphim Order to deal with tha Reapers and their creatures. Tha blades are made of a Fae metal, called Atrum, found deep within the Living Forest of the northern Kingdom of Isiwen. We commission Fae craftsman ta make them and they imbue tha stones on tha hilt with all four elements, ta ground the hunter in this reality. Lucian probably carries something similar." She looks at me with curiosity. All I can manage is a small shake of my head, not willing to admit my blade was lost to the Shadows. Samson continues, oblivious of my discomfort.

"Recruits are given one on their thirteenth birthday if they are going ta become a part of tha Order. Usually no two are alike and made specifically for tha wielder, yet yer parents had a matching set. It's a wonder ye only knew of the one," Samson says around a mouthful of stew.

Florence's eyes bulge, and she drops her spoon back into her bowl, "Fae are real too?"

"You should see your face," I chuckle and kick Samson under the table.

"Ow, wha'" he kicks me back.

"We shouldn't be speaking of this so publicly," I warn.

"Alrigh', don't get yer panties twisted. It's nah like anyone is listening," but he stops talking and digs back into his meal.

"But honestly, all you took from that is that Fae are real?" I tease Florence. She always picks out the strangest part of a conversation to concentrate on.

"One step at a time, Lucian. I can only take in so many revelations at a time," she teases back. "Although I'm not sure why I'm surprised after everything that has happened," she muses.

We eat in silence for a while, and I try to work through the events of yesterday. First, the rogue I've been tracking for months drags the daughter of two of the most famous hunters into the Shadows without the aid of a gate which I find interesting. Then I come to find that she has been living in complete ignorance of all things related to the Seraphim Order and had night terrors until the untimely deaths of Will and Laila, except for last night's relapse.

After I made my way out of the Shadows six months ago, Kalligan confessed that the Order had been struggling to keep up with the increase in rogue activity. He even admitted that the Stuart's mystery daughter may have something to do with that. We were all shocked to learn of her existence, but their eventual move off the grid more logical. Now it appears the attacks are escalating, and the Reapers have become united with one goal in mind, the death and destruction of the Three Kingdoms.

For the last five years, the Reapers have been terrorizing the land, but Florence and her village remained untouched, unaware of the living nightmare outside their boundaries. It is as though they've been living inside a bubble, isolated from the violence. I can feel something big coming. Something we aren't prepared for.

"That might've been the best damn stew I've had in ages," Samson announces, pulling me out of my reverie, leaning back in his chair and patting his belly.

"That's because you refuse to let me cook for you regularly," Florence tells him. She looks at me and asks, "Can you believe this man?" Pointing her thumb in his direction. "I offer him fine, home cooking and he'd rather go spend his time and hard-earned money supporting, what does he call it, the 'working woman'," she smiles and waggles an eyebrow at me.

My heart skips a beat seeing her smile for the first time. I may have been out of touch with the world for a while, but I'm still a full-blooded male, and I'd have to be blind to not see this girl's beauty. Her green eyes sparkle with mischief, and a light dusting of freckles spill across round cheeks and pert nose, giving her an almost innocent look. Rich brown hair that shines red in the sunlight falls down her back in a thick braid. A strong body with womanly curves. I've seen her run and battle invisible demons. This woman could be a force with a little training.

Her smile fades and I realize I haven't responded, "ah, I see nothing has changed," I smile back. "Still chasing skirts old man?"

Samson sputters, "Old man?! I may be getting on in me years, but I can still take ye. Ye just landed a lucky blow earlier. And I don't see any of those women complaining," he winks at Florence.

"You, yourself said your old bones weren't working like they used to!" I'm having a good laugh now and so is Flor.

When did I start thinking of her as Flor?

"It's different when I say it, lad." He gives me an irritated look, downs the last of his ale and gets up to leave. "I'll be in the stable."

Florence is still giggling as she says, "Now you'll have to apologize for bruising his ego."

She sobers a little, eyes lingering on me, "We really should go. The faster we get the Darkwell the faster we can figure out what is going on."

"Agreed." I throw a few more coppers on the table and we follow Samson to the stable.

Chapter 7
Florence

I trail behind Lucian as we head back to the stable. Mulling over our last exchange, I've decided I can trust him-to an extent. I cannot remember the last time I enjoyed a conversation with someone other than Samson. Lucian has grown from someone I once feared to co-conspirator in a short amount of time.

His looks might've helped sway my opinion of him. Where once I saw an enemy, I now see a friend, a handsome one at that. The depth of his eyes leaves me weak and I itch to run my hands through his unruly dark hair. That masculine jaw and rugged appearance make him a threat to my heart.

Mentally I slap myself for these thoughts. My life has irrevocably changed. I am in mortal danger, and here I am mooning over some stranger.

Scoffing at my wandering eyes, we reach our mounts, and I busy myself tightening the already tight saddle bags. Logically, I know it is because I've been shunned by people my own age for so long that a little attention from anyone other than Samson is nice. And he came to my rescue, twice. Bringing me back from the Shadows and then waking me from my dream.

Silly thoughts for a silly girl. These distractions need pushed to the back of my mind.

Pack secured, I pat my pockets for the note and the dagger then swing myself into the saddle. Riding astride is uncomfortable in a dress, but I've been wearing leggings underneath my skirts lately, so I am not necessarily indecent. The stable boy gives me a funny look but says nothing as Lucian hands down a few coins.

He kicks his Namidian into a trot, and we are off. I ride next to Samson most of the way with Lucian in the lead. His cloak billows out behind him as we pick up the pace. He motions for us to pull up our hoods. The weather is almost too warm for cover, but I understand his caution. We cannot be too careful after I was attacked in broad daylight yesterday.

Samson whistles a tune I know well. A popular song played at most of the bonfires I attended. The upbeat jig could either be danced solo or with a partner. My father usually partnered with me while my mother danced with the other married men and we danced the night away. I grin at the memory and join in, humming the melody.

Lucian looks back at us with a small smile, and my heart picks up tempo. I can feel my cheeks heat and look everywhere but back at him. My gratuitous thoughts have made me shy.

"Yer father loved ta dance with ye ta that song," Samson says dreamily once the song is finished.

"That was one of my favorites. He never let me sit it out." From my chest, a dull ache radiates, my constant companion. I miss my father. He encouraged me to be adventurous and allowed me to play with the boys, told me to get dirty. He taught me that no one is beneath you and if you can help, you should.

I now understand a lot of that stemmed from his past. He wanted me to be strong yet compassionate, courageous and understanding. Lessons I've tried to carry with me despite many personal challenges. The hostility from the locals included. My father would say they are just superstitious country folk who do not know any better. I never held a grudge nor blamed them for their hatred. I still don't. It isn't their fault they didn't understand what was happening to me when I barely understood it myself.

Samson continues to whistle all of my favorites. I know what he is doing. He is trying to offer me a little comfort and apologize for keeping so many secrets. While he simultaneously played a part in this chaotic turn of events, he has been here to see me through it. I'll let him. It is nice to be reminded of a time before the interminable sadness. The inescapable guilt I carry about the death of my parents. Of a time before I had to learn to exist on my own. He has been my solid foundation for the last five years, and I'm not sure what I would have done without him.

We spend a majority of the ride this way, Samson whistling while Lucian and I listen contently.

The sun begins its slow decent into the horizon, ending another day. I can smell wood smoke and incense on the breeze. We must be closing in on Wolfewater.

Lucian slows down and draws even with us as the road widens. The town appears to be no more than an extended outpost. Buildings hastily erected to accommodate the increasing number of travelers. As the Kingdoms became allies and began openly trading, the number of goods circulating dramatically increased. This meant more business for merchants and opportunities for those looking to cash in on this expanding market.

The longer the trade route, the greater the need for places to find a meal and a bed. Finding a body to warm the bed was an added bonus. Madams moved their harems to these outposts and brothels became more prolific along popular routes. Thus, Wolfewater was born, where you can find a meal, a bed and a body all in one place. There are others like it littered across the Three Kingdoms and I would bet that they all look similar.

We pass underneath a wooden sign, swaying under the fading light. Burnt into the wood is the image of a wolf, head and front legs stretched upward away from the swells of a river. A shudder passes through my body. I look at Lucian from the corner of my eye to see if he detected anything strange, but his eyes are trained on something in the distance, jaw clenched.

Samson continues to whistle as we make our way down the main thoroughfare. Women in revealing corsets lean against doorways and hang out of windows. Dirt streaked travelers disappear into darkened taverns and wagons laden with supplies amble through the streets. The town may not be overly large, but it is a bustling with activity.

There are a few tradesmen scattered amongst the inns and taverns. A repair shop for wagons that may need a new wheel, a leather shop and a small smithy that could handle horseshoes and any smaller request.

Lucian leads us about halfway through town before dismounting in front of a quaint establishment. The entryway is a vibrant red, a small brown barrel painted in the center. Bronze letters above the door read The Barrel House, blazing in the evening glow. Flower boxes sit on either side of the door and tulips spring from rich earth. Orange, yellow and pink blooms decorate an otherwise muddy palate. Tulips would grace the hillsides around

Grimsfield this time of year, but I've never seen someone cultivate their beauty in this fashion.

I quickly dismount so that I can take a closer look. The center of the orange blooms are dotted with a purple color that is almost black. What an interesting design. Maybe the owner of the tavern can tell me what creates this pattern. I do love flowers. Especially tulips. We may suffer the harshest of winters, but these flowers will still rise from their cold graves to greet the spring.

They will grow despite the decay in their way, proving stronger than the elements. Heralding a new season, a new start, a fresh chance to flourish and shake off the deadend remains of what they once were.

Distracted as I am by the flowers, I almost lose track of my cohorts. The door is already closing behind them when I catch a glimpse of Samson's cloak. Touching the petal of the orange blossom goodbye, I walk through the entrance.

This can't be right.

The scent of pine is overwhelming, and the only thing I can see in all directions are towering evergreens. Behemoth trees dwarf me, their trunks as thick as houses. I crane my neck but cannot the tops. Uniform branches weighed down by heavy needles interlock overhead blocking out any natural light. Small glowing orbs dart through the limbs, creating a hazy light. I turn back toward the door only to see a thick layer of vines crawling over the surface. Samson and Lucian are nowhere in sight.

"This isn't the strangest thing you've seen recently. Breathe." I tell myself while moving amidst the trees. Brown needles cushion my steps, making my progress almost silent. The glowing orbs hover in front of me, lighting my way through the maze.

Soft music twirls a lazy melody ahead of me, and I can make out lanterns strung beneath the trees' canopy. Broken pine needles give way to vibrant rugs and gauzy linens. I have read about gypsy encampments but have never seen one in person. Tents of all sizes dot the small oasis. A trio of violins cry a melancholy tune, and fire crackles from a pit surrounded by lavish cushions.

Large sticks of incense encircle the seating area, clouding the air with patchouli. I find it rather pleasant compared to the sterile pine.

Seated across the fire is a woman covered in Eastern garb. Teal and silver gossamer robes wrap around her lithe body. Namidian dress is light and loose to suit their equestrian lifestyle. Namid is the eastern most realm in the Three Kingdoms and breeds the best horses, like the one Lucian rides.

The woman's ebony hair is braided down her back with glass beads woven throughout. Her pointed ears are showing, and I know immediately she must be Fae. She doesn't look like the Fae in the stories I used to read, all washed out and bright. She is exotic and untamed. The Eastern dress suits her dark features. A crown of flowers sits along her tan brow and silver eyes which match her attractive clothing flash in my direction.

I still cannot find the source of the haunting music and see no other being around, yet I feel at ease. Floating toward the fire, my eyes grow heavy.

I just need a little rest. If I lay down for a moment, the fatigue will wear off.

The fire is warm, and the pillows are so inviting. Have I ever been to a more divine place?

I could stay here forever.

This woman is so beautiful. She watches me lazily, a smile in her dancing eyes. I know she would care for me.

"Sit down, Florence Stuart. Give me your burdens," the gypsy beckons.

"Yes. Yes, I will," I whisper, sinking into the plush cushions. I lay my head down and gaze at my hostess, "Tell me your name," I plead.

"You may call me Lilyera."

"Lilyera," I echo. "It does not sound as pretty when I say it."

Her laugh is like wind chimes is the rain, lovely and violent. I give her a toothy grin and start to forget all my worries.

Wasn't I looking for someone?

I can't remember. Nothing matters but this enchanting beauty before me.

"Tell me, sweetling, what has brought you here?" She reaches a bejeweled hand toward a bowl of fruit, selecting a ripe grape. Slowly, she raises it to her cupid's bow lips and places it into her mouth. I'm not sure I've ever seen someone eat a simple grape more seductively. My mouth waters as I watch her chew.

Swallowing, I place my fingertips against my own lips, voice hoarse when I answer, "I don't know. I opened a door, and here you were. Although, I'm not even sure where here is."

"You are in the Living Forest of Isiwen, my home." Lilyera says it matter-of-factly, as if she didn't just inform me I am in a different Kingdom hundreds of miles away from Wolfewater.

The fog in my head starts to clear, and I sit up straight. "What?" I cry.

Leveling her metallic gaze on me she looks unaffected by my outburst. "My tulips granted you access to my sanctuary. You must have need of me." Picking through the fruit bowl again, she finds what she is looking for, a golden apple, and takes a bite.

I forget myself watching her and don't respond for several minutes. She seems content to let me look and does not speak again.

"How is this possible?" I ask, reevaluating my surroundings. There is a dream-like quality to this place. The music seems to come from everywhere at once, wrapping around my body, seeking entry. The moving lights continue to dance through the air. One flits in front of my face, and in an instant, trails away, a bell like trill left in its wake.

Pixies. I've read about them in stories, fairytales, never once believing them to exist.

Again, not the strangest thing I've seen. I am among the Fae. You can taste the magic in the air, cloying like the patchouli from the incense. Maybe the incense is magic.

I still cannot make sense of how I got here.

"You must be so tired, sweetling," Lilyera says after swallowing a bite of apple. "Your journey is far from over, and you've a great purpose you must fulfill. Rest."

My eyelids begin to droop drowsily once again. My bones are heavy. So heavy. My skull must weigh at least 20 stone.

The music quiets, and the warmth from the fire relaxes my muscles. Mustn't forget my purpose, I think. But what purpose?

The last thing I see before I give into the lull is Lilyera settling a thick blanket over my prone form. Her soft voice follows me under, "Give me your dreams."

Deep breaths. Deeps breaths.

I can just make out hushed conversation as I resurface.

"Is she going to be all right?"

"What happened?"

"Lilyera, happened."

"Who?"

I recognize that name.

Prying my eyelids open, Lucian's face reels into focus.

I could get used to this. Waking to see those eyes looking at me. Touching each part of my face, cataloging my features, memorizing their shape.

My lips tug up at the edges, groggily smiling at him I reach my fingers toward his face. "So perfect," I trace his strong chin. Electricity zips under my skin and his eyes briefly glow.

A throat clears and my eyes pop fully open. Wide-awake, and exceedingly embarrassed, I snatch my hand back. A blush heats my neck and I sit up while Lucian hastily moves out of my space.

"Wha' did tha' she-witch want with ye?" Samson huffs at me from next to the window. We are in a small room that has a table for two, a hearth and a bed stuffed with moss. The room must be upstairs because all I can see is blackness through the window pane. I must have been gone longer than I thought. Lucian takes a seat at the table, water basin and a tray of meats, cheese and nuts crowd the surface.

"Where are we?" Is all I can ask, placing my feet flat on the floor. My head pounds and I need water. A thin layer of film has coated the inside of my mouth. I need to rinse it out, now.

"We are in a room at The Barrel House. You didn't follow us inside, and when I went to find you, you were gone. Vanished. Samson noticed the flowers outside and knew immediately what happened. We've been waiting in this room for you to come back." Lucian glances toward the place Samson occupies, "I guess this is where Lilyera returns her visitors."

"Lilyera," I roll her name. Remembering her flashing eyes and beautiful face makes me shiver. "I found her in a clearing and she asked me for my dreams. She said we were in Isiwen..."

Samson makes a sound in the back of this throat, striding toward me, "Dreams? A ploy ta make you stay. Ye need ta be a wee less curious lass, she coulda kept ye there fer eternity. Damn Fae and their tricks. Lilyera has been known to acquire mortal pets, yer lucky she didna find ye more appealing."

I don't tell him I could have stayed there forever, to let her give me everything I've ever wanted. I felt safe. Protected. Magic, it seems, can control your desires, your fears and I couldn't help my reaction to it, my need for her comfort even now. I will never forget those eyes, or her striking beauty, nor will I forget that I have a purpose. One beyond my own needs. I don't have a clue what it is yet, but my visit with Lilyera, brief as it may have been, re-centered my axis.

Things are changing, in this world and within me, but that does not mean I cannot conquer it.

"It's fine Samson. She let me go. I am whole." Mostly. "Can I have some water, please?" The taste in my mouth is almost unbearable. Grapes and smoke.

Lucian brings me a cup and the pitcher which is a good thing since I finish the first in one gulp. Refilling the cup, I drink this one more slowly while observing Samson. He is fuming, anger leaking into his stilted movements. I'm not sure if his ire is directed at me or Lilyera, but I refuse to be cowed and try to change the subject. "Where will we stay for the remainder of the night?"

"You'll be staying here," answers Lucian. "Samson and I are sharing the room across the hall. Try not to walk into any more Fae traps, alright?" He jokes halfheartedly, forehead creasing with worry.

"I won't be going anywhere," I reassure him, "I just want to eat some of that cheese and go to sleep. Traveling is hard, even when you're just sitting in a saddle all day," I try to ease the tension that is rolling off the two men. All the excitement has worn off and my body has become one giant ache. My legs are raw, and my back may never be right again. Having never ventured far from Grimsfield left me without much riding experience. Sure, I rode on small trips to nearby fields but spending that much time in a saddle makes parts of me hurt that I didn't know could hurt.

Some anger has melted off Samson at my admission and he reaches for the door, "Just keep ta this room. If ye need somethin' we are a short walk away." Hand still holding the knob he stares at me for a moment before giving me a curt nod, "Sleep tight, lass."

I haven't gotten off the bed yet and I'm acutely aware of Lucian's proximity. Abruptly standing I sidle up to the table to pick at the cheese. The air has grown thick and I am still embarrassed by my sleepy confession.

"Do you want me to stay?" I pause my hand midway to my mouth and focus bewildered eyes on his face. Noticing my shock, he clarifies, "At least until you fall asleep? I just want to make sure you will be ok, and I know Samson was really worried about you. He was almost manic while we waited for you to be returned" Ah, so it is to make sure I don't disappear again. He is nothing more than a glorified babysitter.

Playing it cool, I pretend like I wasn't about to shout YES at him and try to imitate the way Lilyera ate. Lucian is watching me with indifference now, distancing himself from the look of concern I saw earlier. Fine. I'll be just as unaffected.

"No, thank you. I'm fine." Abandoning all attempts at eating with grace I shove a few more pieces of cheese in my mouth and walk back to the bed. "Samson snores," I warn as a way of dismissing him, hoping he won't see my disappointment.

"I'll manage," he says awkwardly, still standing in the middle of the room. A look of indecision crosses his face before he sighs and turns toward the door. "Sweet dreams," he utters, and a look of raw desire replaces his indifference right before he shuts the door.

What am I supposed to do with that?

I fling myself down atop the scratchy coverlet. Sleep is next to impossible now that my pulse is ricocheting off my skin.

Deep breaths. Take deep breaths.

I imagine I am back with Lilyera, listening to the haunting violins, the music both sad and soothing. She sings me to sleep, pulling the delusions from my subconscious, locking them away for her to keep.

Soon I feel the sweet embrace of slumber and hope I'm too tired to dream.

Chapter 8
Florence

A dreamless sleep was too much to hope for.

Instantly I recognize this for what it is, a nightmare. I am out of practice but that feeling of deep desperation is never far from the surface.

The heels of my boots click against the wood floor. An endless hallway. No doors. No windows. No escape.

There has to be an end. If I keep going, I will end up somewhere. I have to. This cannot be forever.

Another pair of boots echo down the hallway. Almost in time with mine but slightly off, so I'll know they are there. I do not speed up or slow down. If I stay in time, they will never catch me.

Again, how could I have been so wrong? The walls melt away and a tall figure joins me as I walk.

"It's a fine evening for a rogue," a rough voice murmurs.

That it is. Twilight has fallen, and a purple haze has settled over the land. We walk in silence, into the void between day and night. The earth takes unsettled breaths as the unknown begins to stir. You can hear it move, seep, become. This is the witching hour, and here we stand, in the thick of it all.

I turn toward my companion and watch with a wild fascination as they lower their hood. Lilyera's face greets me with an impish grin.

"Let's play," she says but with a voice not her own. Smoke billows out of her robes as her smile widens and limbs elongate. Towering above me is a caricature of the beautiful Fae. Her mouth unhinges like that of a snake, and her bony arms sweep me into an embrace.

I can hear things slither out of the darkness, wailing in the throes of chaos. Her arms slowly tighten around me, and it is difficult to breathe, her mouth opening wider.

I am going to be eaten by a grisly version of Lilyera. I know it as certain as I know my own name.

Wake up.

Somehow my dagger ends up in my hand. I brandish the weapon as best I can while being constricted. Lilyera hisses and suddenly I'm dropped to the ground. Blue-white light glows from a small wound in her side and she snaps at me, her mouth crowded with teeth. She laughs, a deep, low-pitched sound that sends goosebumps up my arms.

Her unhinged jaw forms words I can barely understand. Watching her overly-large mouth move is horrifying as the skin on her face sloughs off. Smoke engulfs her, and she dematerializes, black orbs escaping toward the night sky.

Finally, I catch her words, "Wake up, Florence."

I swing my arm out and end up launching my upper half of the bed. With a grunt I catch myself before I fall completely out of the cot. My dagger is clutched in my right hand, and I recognize the room inside The Barrel House from my awkward position partially on the floor. Righting myself I make sure I haven't drawn any blood in my sleep.

I seem to be well enough yet sweat has stuck my clothes to my body. I didn't bother to take off my leggings or my dress, and I regret that decision. It is still dark outside as I peel off my outer layers. I untie the front stays of my dress and drape it over one of the chairs tucked under the table. My leggings go over the other, and I'm left standing in just a shift.

I pile my hair atop my head, getting it off my neck, and open the window to let in the breeze. Tremors dance across my damp skin. Closing my eyes, I try to shake the nightmare loose. Flashes of Lilyera's skin flaking off make my stomach roil. She couldn't mess with my mind like this, could she?

She did say to give her my dreams. But this was something else.

A familiar undercurrent accompanied this slide through madness. The only color came from the gash in the monster's side. Made with my dagger. I eye it, laying atop the uncomfortable coverlet. I don't remember ever waking up with it before, but this is only the second time I've been able to recall what happened during a dream.

Curious.

Maybe I should wake up Samson, see what he thinks. The longer I am awake, the stranger the dream becomes. More abstract and less concrete. The terror won't abate, but I don't feel the immediate need to check under the bed for what lurks in the shadows.

Answers lie in Darkwell. By nightfall tomorrow I'll know what is happening, I can be patient until then.

What I really need now is a bath and a cup of tea. Or whiskey. Definitely whiskey. I'm not usually one to drink, but I think the circumstances call for one, or several.

Too bad it is still the middle of the night.

Sleep is no longer an option. I could explore the inn but the thought of putting my damp clothes back on makes me cringe.

The dagger snags my attention again, and I light the candle next to the bed to peer at the jewels in the handle. Such beautiful craftsmanship. The blade is still sharp and the hilt swirls with color. Atrum is an impressive metal. I cannot believe the elements have been imbued into the weapon. Yet today, I've met a Fae sorceress and came out unscathed.

Anything is possible.

The door knob to my room turns and instinctively I raise the blade. Lucian pokes his head around the door, eyes meeting mine.

"I- I saw the light. Under the door," he stammers, slowly taking in the rest of me. I feel his assessment like a caress and remember that I'm in nothing but a shift and my underthings. My hair is an unkempt mess, wild from the sweat. Quickly dropping the knife, I subtly try to use the blanket to cover myself even though it is pointless now.

"I had a nightmare," is all I can manage.

His heated look cools, and he lets himself the rest of the way in. "You woke yourself up?" He sounds rather impressed, and I tamp down the urge to preen.

"I think I remembered the trick I used to use to wake myself up-before they stopped." I try to sound nonchalant, but his intrusion has me shook. The chairs are occupied by my clothes, so he has nowhere to sit, other than my bed. I pull my feet up to my chest, so he has somewhere to go, other than standing in my doorway.

Gracefully, he sits down on the edge and waits for me to continue.

"My dreams would always be in black and white until I found a spot of color. It could be anywhere. I would use this," I hold up the Seraphim Blade, "to pry open that sliver of brightness and then I would wake up. I wouldn't remember anything except that part, my hands empty and my parents there to comforting me. I never actually held a blade in my hand when I woke until now."

"That you can remember," he says gently.

"That I can remember," I repeat.

"Where did you find it this time?" He asks.

"On Lilyera. But it wasn't Lilyera. It was something horrible that wore her face and tried to eat me. Its mouth... and teeth..." I stop myself. The dream will plague me, just like the dead man's eyes. Maybe it was for the best I couldn't remember anything after I woke, too much to carry.

"Shh, you are here now. You fought your way out," Lucian eases.

"I guess you are right. I couldn't go back to sleep, so I lit a candle, banishing the rest of the dream. And now here you are. What were you doing in the hallway?" I bashfully play with the end of the blanket I now have pulled up to my chest. Selfishly hoping he was watching my door, thinking of me.

"Couldn't sleep either, I guess. I saw your light flicker on and wanted to make sure you were ok," he gives me a sheepish look, almost guilty.

"Thank you, I appreciate it," I say, genuinely grateful he thought to check on me. "How much longer until morning?"

"Not too long I should imagine. Enough time to get a little more rest," he presses.

"I don't think -" but he cuts me off.

"You need to try. We have another long day of riding."

Not appreciating being bossed around, I fold my arms and glare at him. He doesn't move a muscle. A challenge in his eyes.

"Fine," I say, but end up smiling.

"If you don't mind I'll be setting your leggings aside and taking up residence in this chair, hm." Carefully he moves my things and takes root. I don't ask whether he needs more rest, he wouldn't be here if he did. He has seen things I could never dream of, his motives are his own and his presence is comforting, but I will never admit it.

Sleep comes easier this time, and I don't resist the fall once it calls to me.

LUCIAN

I watch her snuggle back into bed, safe inside her blankets. I don't admit I've been watching her door since I left, that her cries during sleep almost broke me, that I heard her fall out of bed and light the candle. I know what it is like to battle invisible demons. I beat them into submission every day.

She has somehow burrowed underneath my skin. It is reckless, yet she is my responsibility. Kalligan deemed it so. But she is becoming more than an assignment, and I cannot stop the tide. Her touch from earlier has seared itself into my memory. Lightning crackled through my frame and I want nothing more than for her to touch me again. The way her eyes softened stopped my heart.

I know she is attracted to me but tries to hide it. That makes her even more alluring. I am bewitched.

Sitting watch the rest of the night, I let foolish thoughts invade my head and hope they dissipate come morning.

FLORENCE

Lucian is nowhere to be found when I wake again. It is for the best; he is an unnecessary distraction and only my handler, nothing more.

Sunlight streams in through the window and a kettle of tea sits on the table.

Bless the Three Kingdoms for that tea.

I dress and pour myself a mug, inhaling the herbs. Everything is always better with tea.

Samson shouts through the door. We need to be off and I down the rest of my breakfast. The tea must've been there a while, it is warm but not scalding so it is easy to finish.

Slamming my feet into my boots, I tuck the dagger away and throw my cloak over my shoulders.

Today I get answers.

I take the stairs two at a time and meet the gentleman downstairs.

"Yer chipper," Samson notes, tightening his laces.

"Just ready to be off," I say, avoiding Lucian. I still can't believe he saw me in nothing but my shift. He seems unaffected this morning, striding out the door toward what I assume is the stables.

"Let's get on with it then," he says, leading me outside.

We mount up and soon leave the makeshift town of Wolfewater in our wake. I wish I had seen more of it but had enough excitement for one visit.

We stop midday to eat a small lunch Samson packed. More cheese, nuts and some dried meat. He must have purchased the meat before we set out. We don't usually have it stocked at the haberdashery. Smart man he is, always prepared, in any situation.

This portion of the trip is rather boring. No one speaks, tired as we are, and there is nothing but forest surrounding us. Eventually the trees break apart to reveal fields tended by locals. This must mean we are closing in on Darkwell, and I perk up a bit.

Around late afternoon, Lucian sits up a little straighter in the saddle. "Do you smell that," he asks.

"Smell what?" I lift my face to the breeze and breathe deep. "I can't smell anything besides excrement from the fields and the occasional hearth fire."

"Yes, fire. It doesn't smell like just hearth fire. There is something underneath it, like charred flesh."

I ride up next to Lucian, and he turns his full gaze on me. "Like charred flesh? Someone is probably just cooking dinner. It is almost time for the evening meal and we are getting closer to the city," I say, trying to dampen the alarm creeping into my voice.

"There is a difference between the smell of animal flesh and human flesh burning, Flor, trust me." Lucian turns faces forward and starts to gallop faster.

We crest the top of a small hill and that's when I smell it. The acrid scent of burning flesh and decaying bodies. My eyes start to water, and I cover my mouth with my hand.

Laid out before us is carnage like I have never seen. For miles, reaching out to the coast, all you can see is scorched earth and blackened buildings. Bodies are strewn everywhere outside the city wall and the rubble of Darkwell smolders in the dying light.

"Sweet heavens," breathes Samson.

I say nothing and sneak a glance at Lucian, a muscle ticking in his jaw. "Reapers," he snarls. "Multiple, it would seem."

Finally, I find my voice, "We have to see if anyone is still alive."

"How did we no' hear of this?" Samson asks at the same time.

"Tread carefully, it will be dusk soon, and we need to find shelter quickly in case anything is still lurking in the city," Lucian commands. "I don't know how they overtook a whole town, but it seems whatever they've been planning has been set in motion."

We pick our way down the hill past burnt crops and charred bodies. The urge to run away and never look back is almost overwhelming. I am keeping a tight leash on my panic as sorrow washes over me. All these innocent lives lost to a war they didn't know was coming. Or maybe they did, and my parents kept such a tight-lipped control on my life I was the only one ignorant to this terror. Unchecked anger and shame grip me. Maybe if I hadn't been born my parents would've kept fighting and this could have been avoided. My life is not worth this much death. I know an irrational part of me as taken over, but I cannot rationalize this much loss.

Crossing under the battlements at the city entrance is a surreal experience. There is no hailing call from the guard post. No sound except the wind whistling through stagnant streets. Our horses' hooves break up the silence when we hit the cobbled street, sounding like gongs ringing in my ears.

Lucian speaks softly, "Move swiftly. We will head for Kalligan's Keep on the east side of the city."

Small fires still burn in some of the storefronts we pass, ash raining from the sky like snow. Doors and windows are smashed inward. Clothes and half packed bags are scattered haphazardly in entryways. We are on high alert for any movement, friendly or foe. Smoke clogs in the back of my throat and I almost gag on the scent of burnt hair. My senses are assaulted with the sights and smells of death. Deep furrows mar the side of houses.

"What made those marks?" I ask Lucian.

"Lyall. Monstrous black wolves with two tails from the Shadow Territories," he says looking over the scratches. "Nasty, ill-tempered beasts, very loyal to a Reaper if bonded to it. Legend has it that the original Lyall started out as a normal wolf. But he had a brother who was stronger, quicker and more vicious than he. His jealously over his brother's power consumed him, and he sought out the Reapers to help him. One Reaper took pity on his plight and shared his ability to harvest souls. This gave the wolf the skills to absorb his brother's strength. The next morning, the jealous wolf crept up to his brother while he was resting and inhaled his essence, leaving nothing behind. With this new soul, he grew in stature and inherited in all of his brother's coveted traits. And thus, a new, monstrous breed was created. The only sign of his brother's existence was the second tail that grew from his backside. A constant reminder of what he had done. So grateful he was for the Reaper's help he bonded with the creature and pledged to work by his side for the rest of his days."

"Sounds lovely," I deadpan. We keep moving forward, and I focus my eyes straight ahead, I do not wish to see the mangled corpses. A man who has been ripped in half lies next to a woman clutching a scorched child in her arms. Tears blaze a trail down my cheeks, and I cough on soot. We are riding through a living hell. The eerie silence of a forsaken town our only company. These people suffered so at the end. Where was Kalligan and the Order? Why didn't they stop this?

Gasping suddenly, I pull my mount to a halt. I've been here. I've run for my life through these streets. A makeshift platform stands in the city center. A man in clerics robes is on his knees, run through with a spear in the spot a Reaper stood, pointing me to the tower with the hanging man.

"What is it lass?" Samson asks pulling up beside me.

I turn a frightened stare on him and utter, "this is where I was two nights ago. In my dream. I was running through these streets." I indicate to the platform, "that is where the Reaper stood and pointed to the man swinging from the tower."

"Maybe it's no' the same, just a coincidence."

"No, I know this is where I was Samson, something chased me through these streets."

We gradually move around the building that is blocking our view, like it was in my dream. I look up toward the tower I know will be there and see a man hanging from the ramparts. His eyes are gone, and his face is purple and puffy from swinging on the end of the rope. Stifling a scream, I round on Samson, hysteria making my movements frantic.

His face is bleached white and his mouth hangs open. I'm yelling now, "I saw this man! I was looking at this very man before Lucian woke me." I clutch his arm, breath sawing in and out of my lungs.

I think I might pass out when Lucian speaks, "that man you saw in your dreams and who is hanging here now is who we came all this way to see."

My head snaps in his direction, "What?"

"That man was the leader of the Seraphim Order, and his name was Kalligan."

Chapter 9
Lucian

Two things became very clear to me the moment I see Kalligan's lifeless body dangling above us. The first one being that all-out war has come down on the Three Kingdoms, and that no one, not even the leader of the Order, is safe. The second and probably more interesting of the two, is that Florence is anything but a regular girl.

"Should we cut 'im down?" Samson asks while staring blank faced at the body.

"We need to see if there is anything left of the Order before we go climbing towers," I say. It sounds cold, but night is swiftly approaching, and we need to get indoors. Hopping off Javai, I nod that the other two should follow suit.

Kalligan's Keep is an extension of the outer wall, connecting to the tower where his body hangs. The main entrance is blocked by overturned, burnt carts and part of what used to be a bookstore directly across the street. Unfortunately, there is nowhere safe to tie the horses, we have to hope they don't roam too far from the Keep. Shouldering our packs, I give the horses instructions to stay close, knowing my request may fall on deaf ears.

Samson eyes the charred mass in front of the entrance, "How do ye suppose we'll get in? I'm nah sure the three of us can move tha' mess."

"There are less-public ways to enter the Keep, my friend." Stepping over fallen beams, I lead us around the rubble in front of the door and follow the wall to around to the right. One hundred meters past the entrance, we come upon a rather large, half-moon shaped drain in the bottom of the wall. It looks just like every other sewer drain spaced out evenly along the wall. Each one leads to a network of tunnels under the city. This one, however, leads directly into the basement of the Keep. Kalligan liked to think it was hidden in plain sight and could be used in an emergency situation. Either the city was ambushed before he could use the exit, or like a good captain, went down with the ship.

Prying loose the grate I motion for Samson to go first. "There is about a three-meter drop," I warn.

"Yer certainly full of surprises, lad. I take it this leads into the bowel of tha Keep?"

"Yes, and the rest of the city if you know how to navigate the labyrinth of tunnels." Handing Samson down I reach for Flor who looks like she would rather have her teeth pulled.

"I don't like cramped spaces," she says as she hesitantly takes a step toward me.

"You can walk away from a nightmare unscathed, and face down death and destruction but the thought of a tight space makes you hesitate?" I tease her, trying to see any hint of a smile.

"No one is perfect," she huffs and drops into the tunnel without my help.

Landing beside Flor we double back towards the street entrance. There is still enough daylight coming in through the openings to guide us to the underground door. Shrapnel from snapped beams and singed cloth drift through the water running down the middle of the tunnel.

I can feel Florence's body heat to my left as she keeps pace with me. I don't comment on her nearness for fear she will move away. Whispering into my shoulder she asks, "How exactly are we going to get into the basement? It doesn't look like there is a door anywhere."

Pulling her to a stop, I make sure Samson is with us. That man can be uncannily stealthy when he wants to be, but I guess that's what made him such an effective hunter. "Look at the wall here. Notice the pattern of the stones as they alternate vertically. But here, these two are side by side." Running my hand over the stones I stop about waist high where two sit parallel. "These two stones mirror one another and indicate our way in. See," I take Flor's hand in mine and press it to the left stone, dragging her fingers toward the middle. As they move so does the stone, rotating inward to reveal a catch in the right stone. "Go on, pull."

She does, and a door sized chunk of wall swings outward.

"Clever," she remarks, examining the opposite side of the door. "You can't even see the hinges."

"Ingenious design to make sure there are no unwanted visitors. All manner of ruffians utilize these sewers to move about the city unseen."

"And yet, against all odds, you found the way in," Florence observes. Samson barks a laugh and disappears into the basement.

"It would seem that way," I quirk a brow at her, deciding I like this playful side. "After you," I challenge, testing her bravado. She makes a small sound in the back of her throat like she might protest but brushes past me and dematerializes in the dark.

Shutting the door behind us, I turn to face the room. The strike of flint on steel disrupts the silence. Sparks jump, igniting a candle wick that illuminates the basement.

We are not alone.

Five weapons of various shapes and sizes are aimed in our direction, wielded by five angry looking survivors. Flor and Samson both raise their hands in surrender, and I reach for the blade on my hip.

"I wouldn't be doing that if I were you, hunter," the one in the middle speaks. Four men and one woman form a semi-circle around us, penning us in. Quickly, I scan each person, evaluating the threat level. They all hold a custom Seraphim Blade and I slowly hold my palms out in front of me.

"Apologies for the intrusion, but this is the only way into the Keep as the main gate has been blocked. We traveled from Grimsfield, two days ride west of here, to speak with Kalligan. But it would seem we arrived too late. My name is Lucian Campbell of the Seraphim Order, this is Samson MacDuff formerly of the same Order and Florence Stuart, daughter of William and Laila Stuart."

Lowering their weapons, the man in the middle speaks again, "No shite, we heard you were coming this way. I didn't recognize ya Samson, it's me, Thierry," he smiles. "Retirement has made you a little soft round the middle, eh? And a pleasure to finally meet you Florence."

"I knew it was ye, ye idiot. Couldna verra well speak while you had a sword in me face." Samson embraces the man called Thierry, and the other four sheathe their weapons. "And I'm no' soft, there is just more a me ta go 'round."

"Come, sit. You're certainly a sight for sore eyes." Thierry settles himself on a crate while the others scatter throughout the room, lighting more candles. I choose to stay standing by the doorway and keep a close eye on Florence who is moving about the space. She keeps glancing in my direction and I think it is to make sure she knows where I am. I don't move. I'd rather be by the exit anyway, just in case things go south.

Once there is enough light to see everyone clearly, Thierry introduces us to the others. Pointing to a man who appears to be in his late thirties with a dirty bandage wrapped around his head and bloody clothes, "This here is Gregg. He took a nasty blow to the skull. That mean looking fella there is Wallace, and over by the door are Aggie and Aric, twins from the North. We are all that seem to be left alive here at the Keep."

"Wha' in tha name of tha Three Kingdoms happened here, Thierry? We rode into a massacre with no warning."

"It all happened so fast we lost track of who was dying. The gate that Kalligan sealed all those years ago has been reopened. Something broke through the barrier from the inside, once we realized what was happening, it was too late. We were overrun. There were at least six Reapers and their pack of wolves," he explains.

"Did anythin' else come through? And what about Kalligan-how did he end up on the wrong end of a rope?"

Thierry swallows and casts Samson a look of regret, "He was in the room when the gate exploded open. I was out on an errand and late getting back... I've should've been there when it happened. He told Aggie and Aric to run and barred the door. His sacrifice bought 'em enough time to get out. They found me and Gregg in the hallway after the initial explosion, shook the whole building it did. Gregg took a nice tumble down the stairs from the tower, smashed his head real good. As far as anything else getting through, we haven't detected any disturbances. We think the goal was to create chaos and send the Order and the rest of the Kingdoms a message: We no longer control the gates. The beasts tore through the city so fast we didn't have time to issue a warning. We've been holed up down here since the attack a couple nights ago. Things seem quiet on the surface, but you'd know better than us. Aric and Aggie have been scouting the tunnels to see if anyone else made it underground. That's why that door still opens. So far, we found Wallace and several pockets of survivors, but we estimate it isn't more than 50 people. Those who had access close to their homes or businesses and knew to get below ground were able to make an escape. The Reapers set fire to everything they could. You know how quick those thatch roofs catch, spread like a plague. I can still hear the screams," he shudders.

Flor comes back to stand beside me and asks what I've been wondering myself, "Do you think this was a singular attack or is it possible some of the other gates were ambushed as well?"

"Based on the number of Reapers that came through, I am thinking it was a concentrated attack, but that doesn't mean there aren't more planned. They needed to consolidate their strength in order to get that gate open, and since this is more or less home base for the Order, it makes logical sense they would strike here first. Also, most of our hunters are out tracking the increased number of rogues which meant the city was left virtually defenseless. This is an organized onslaught."

"This is why ye shoulda been tha Order's strategist, Thierry. That brain a yers has already worked through tha finer points despite tha crisis tha' just occurred," Samson chimes in. "We dinna seen anythin' but tha smoldering ruins of tha city as we rode through. I assume tha' means tha Reapers, and tha Lyall went back through the gate."

"Or they moved on to terrorize another town," Florence says to Samson.

"Nay, they canna exist outside tha Shadows for extended periods o' time. Too long and they become phantoms, incorporeal spirits stuck in a sorta limbo. Tha power within the Territories keeps them tangible."

"Why are they doing this? Aren't there enough souls of the dying they can collect?"

"Tha souls of tha dying donna feed into the dark magic tha Reapers wield or tha power of their land, they are released to travel into the next life and donna linger in tha Shadows. Tha souls of the living, however, become trapped in tha void with tha Reaper who plucked them from this life. There, tha souls are fed on, making those monsters stronger. That is why we track down the rogues who steal those living souls. Not only because of the power side effects, but to become trapped in tha Shadows is its own kind of torment," Samson casts me a look that borders on pity but quickly looks away. He knows I don't want his pity.

"That's terrible," she squeaks.

I can feel Florence's eyes on the side of my face, and my temples start to pound. I don't want her pity either. Clearing my throat, I take a few steps away from her, "By now, it is full dark out. We need a plan, and we need a place to stay. Can we bunk with you five tonight? In the morning, we can plan accordingly. I think our best shot is to stick together, maybe get the rest of the survivors out of the tunnels when it is daylight and see if we can't contact anyone at the other gates."

"That's a good plan," Gregg agrees. "Besides, I need someone to re-wrap this bandage and would like a moments rest before all hell breaks loose again. Maybe find that wine stash I know is down here."

"Here, here!" Samson cheers, eagerly checking through crates and corners for the home-brew. "Also, has anyone seen me bird?"

"Inna flew off when the barrier burst," the woman named Aggie drawls, picking at her fingernails with a blade.

"Shame that, good bird," Samson doesn't sound sad at the loss of his messenger, which I find a little strange.

"Maybe she will turn up when the dust settles," Thierry offers. "In the meantime, welcome to the Keep."

Chapter 10
Florence

The basement is little more than a collection of supplies and rooms for storage. We are in the largest space crammed with crates of miscellaneous items. The stairs leading up to the Keep are through a narrow hallway opposite the door we came through. Wallace told me that in the event of an emergency, a steel slab can be dropped behind the door leading from the Keep into the basement. There is a lever at the bottom of the stairs that operates the pulley. This effectively seals out any threat, but it also seals anything in. That was why a hidden door was placed down here as an escape route.

Dried meats and jarred goods take up most of what appears to be a root cellar off of this room. Closets full of weapons, explosives, parchment, candles, linens and medicinal supplies line the hallway. There could be worse places to be stuck during an attack. Clearly the Order kept this place well stocked in case the city ever fell.

The thick limestone walls seep with moisture, making the air smell damp and rotten. Torches spaced out throughout the basement remain unlit until we absolutely need them, but the candle supply hasn't been so lucky.

I watch Aric re-bandage Gregg's head, trying to remember the few healing skills my mother taught me.

Fortunately, the cut is shallow so there won't be any permanent damage, yet nothing bleeds like a head wound. He will need to have the wrap replaced again in the morning. Samson hands me some water from the barrels in the root cellar and Thierry makes the rounds with rations of dried meat and nuts.

Aggie remains in the corner pouring over an old map weighted down with sacks of sugar. It is the original schematics of the sewers, and they've been using it to systematically comb through the tunnels. Charcoal markings indicate where they've found survivors and where they have already checked.

She and Aric had just returned from a trip when we arrived. They quickly blew out the candles when they heard Lucian and I manipulate the mechanism in the door. No one outside of the Order knows how to work the door, but they didn't want to assume anything in the aftermath of everything that happened. We interrupted her before she was able to finish making her notes.

Lucian is sitting with his back against a crate chewing some dried meat when I plop down next to him. I slosh a little water out of my cup onto my faded blue skirt. It was already in disrepair before this harrowing trip. Now it is beyond help. I shrug and reach over to steal some of his jerky.

"What do you think is going to happen now?" I ask.

Looking at me out of the side of his eye, he takes another bite and remains silent while he eats. He swallows and expels a breath, "I don't know Flor. What is left of the Order here is going to have to call all of those hunters out in the field back to regroup. That is going to take time, and time is something we don't have. They can't very well meet here either. The city has been decimated and now that the gate is open again, who knows what might come through while it is unattended."

"Isn't that more reason to meet here? Once we gain numbers, we can defend the rest of the Kingdoms from whatever else craws through."

"Oh, it's we now is it?" He smiles.

"I can't very well turn back, now can I? You've already dragged me too deep," I say nudging his elbow. "And you've seen what my life was like in Grimsfield. I didn't really have one." I try to laugh, but it comes out stilted, and I look down at my cup. "I need to know what really happened to my parents, Lucian. Now that I know they were fighting Reapers, maybe I can somehow honor their memory but helping you." I take a breath, voicing my real concern, "And I'm starting to think my dreams were never really dreams at all." I chance a look at Lucian for confirmation, but his face is unreadable.

"I have a theory, but my theories usually end up with catastrophic consequences," he says before taking a sip of his water. "That was how I got myself trapped in the first place, testing a theory."

"What happened?" I place my hand on his arm and will him to tell me.

He doesn't look at me as he leans his head back against the crate and stares into his past. "I was young and naive. I believed I had everything all figured out and could outsmart a Reaper," he scoffs, running a hand through his hair.

"My cousin Niall and I were only a few months apart in age and grew up together. We were inseparable and always getting into trouble. We received our first Seraphim Blades at thirteen together and were inducted into the Order when we turned sixteen," he says, smiling at the fond memory. "We weren't allowed to hunt Reapers without a senior member of the Order with us, but we were able to scout out potential rogue sightings, collect intel, that kind of thing. Basically, do most of the groundwork before more experienced hunters would come in and take care of the threat.

"One day, Kalligan sent Niall and I to a town on the border of Namid and Rolum called Hidazad to investigate possible Reaper activity. There is a gate there, and the reports mentioned bodies drained of all fluids, signs a Reaper had taken a soul. He gave us strict orders to not engage should we find the culprit and said he would be dispatching a couple hunters from a nearby city who would join us the following day.

"Once we got to town, we started asking the locals about the reports. They gave us directions to the homes where the sightings and the deaths occurred. Most of the day was spent listening to grieving mothers and outraged townsfolk. You see, we are a dying breed. Most families don't allow their children to pledge themselves to the Order anymore. Too dangerous. There aren't enough members of the Seraphim to go around, and we cannot place a hunter at every gate across the Kingdoms. That means some of the smaller towns have to go without protection, and this one was left unattended. Niall and I received the brunt of their anger over this fact, and they blamed us for what was happening.

"Despite the hostile environment, we did our job. Based on the information we gathered, it sounded like the town had its own personal boogeyman. For seven nights straight, a Reaper would slip into the homes of families who had teenage boys on the verge of adulthood, much like Niall and me. The creature would then relinquish the boys of their souls and flee back to the Shadows. Their families would wake up to the drained bodies, appearing as if their insides were sucked out. The only thing left a husk.

"Our backup wasn't due to arrive until the morning, but we couldn't let this town suffer anymore. I came up with a plan, we would lure the Reaper to us, ambush it and take care of the beast once and for all. Seeing as he went after virile young men, I thought we fit the bill perfectly.

"That night we made sure we stayed somewhere with a direct line of sight to the gate and waited. Around midnight, we saw the Reaper emerge from the rift between this world and the Shadows. Immediately we sprang into action, making enough noise to draw its attention. After it started heading our way, we crouched below the window where we were hiding, weapons at the ready.

"However, we didn't consider how quickly and silently Reapers move. Unable to hear its movements, we thought that maybe it had missed us, continuing on. I motioned for Niall to look, and as he began to rise, an arm darted through the window and pulled him through before I could react. I dove out trying to grab on to him, but the Reaper was too quick. I watched in shock as that-that thing drank Niall dry. His soul was a beautiful and brilliant white cloud swallowed into the black abyss of the Reapers hood. You would think something like that would come with a sound, but no, the whole process was harshly silent.

"I had miscalculated, and my cousin paid with his life. I lost all sense of reason, and the need for vengeance became a living thing inside me. The Reaper dropped Niall's body before I chased it back toward the gate. He disappeared through the threshold before I could catch him. I wasn't finished with it yet though. Throwing caution to the wind I leapt into the void. The Reaper was on the other side waiting for me to take the bait. Niall's soul lent him strength but my need for blood overrode his desire to kill me. My blade made it across with me and after a short scuffle, I stabbed the Reaper through. The metal of the sword went to work, and it died in a flash of light with a horrible wail. The souls he stole were released into the air on a powerful blast that knocked me unconscious.

"I woke up completely disoriented and alone. I didn't find my way back out until six months ago when I followed the Reaper I've been tracking since I escaped. The same one that found you, Florence. A decade had passed, but it felt like an eternity. Time moves differently in the Shadows. You are unaware of it passing."

Lucian falls silent, and I realize everyone in the room has been listening. Six of us holding a collective breath.

"No one has gone through a gate and survived," Gregg's revelation sounds too loud in the wake of this story.

"We dinna know what had happened tha' day or where you had gone. We held a joint funeral for you and Niall, assuming you had been lost as well." He pats Lucian on the shoulder before sitting by Thierry, "I'm so sorry, lad."

"What was it like?" Aric asks quietly.

Closing his eyes, Lucian continues in a small voice, "it was lonely. You are of this world but not part of it. The cold is unrelenting and bone deep. All colors are a muted gray, and it is as if you are a ghost. You can see this world but not the people within it. I eventually learned that if it has a soul, you cannot see it while you're in the Shadows, I think that is why the Reapers crave them." He opens his eyes and looks at me as if to ground himself, "I wasn't able to eat, yet I somehow did not die. My organs were stagnant, but I continued to develop on the outside. I assume the magic that fuels the Shadows has something to do with that.

"I stole the clothes from the Reaper I killed to blend into the environment," he holds up the front of his cloak, poking his fingers through the tear where he stabbed the Reaper through. "At first I attempted to climb back through the gate on my own. Nothing happened. I stayed close to the rift, hoping someone would attempt to find me, but no one did. Those in the Seraphim don't go through the gates, they protect them. I didn't see another Reaper until the day I escaped but as we know, all sorts of things lurk within the Shadows."

Candlelight flickers across Lucian's brow, and I watch him wrestle back his demons. I cannot imagine the things he has seen, the things he has done-or maybe I can. My heart aches for this boy forced to grow up alone, in a foreign land, fighting for his life and a way back home. I squeeze his arm to offer my support, because I know words are insufficient.

I cannot bear to see the sad look in his eyes anymore and ask an innocent enough question, "What was the first thing you ate when you got back?"

"Stew," he says wistfully and the left side of his mouth lifts into a smile. His cheek dimples and I can't help but return the gesture.

"Well, I sure won't be sleeping well tonight," Thierry says, blowing out some of the candles.

I stiffen, and Lucian leans in to speak softly to me, "I'm with you, Flor." More loudly he adds in Thierry's direction, "Maybe leave one burning for now, since we are unfamiliar with the place."

"Good plan Lucian. Can't have you stepping on me when you go to relieve yourself in the middle of the night."

I send a grateful look Lucian's way, soundlessly thanking him.

"The dark can be a terrible place."

I nod in agreement and confess, "I'm afraid to fall asleep. I'm afraid of what I will see."

"I'll be right here to wake you if something happens. Promise. I don't sleep much these days anyway, and someone needs to keep watch."

"Alright," I say. "Maybe just an hour or so."

"Here," he pats his lap. "Rest your head on my leg. That way I'll know for sure if you start dreaming." Sensing my uncertainty, he adds, "It will offer me a small comfort after reliving one of my worst memories."

I can't very well say no to that.

Acquiescing, I scoot down so my head is even with his thigh. Curling onto my side, I pull my hands up under my chin, resting my head on his warm leg. My back tingles when I feel him lightly place a hand at the center of my spine. He is right. This is a small comfort in an otherwise tumultuous time. Becoming drowsy, Lucian lulls me to sleep, rubbing his hand in small circles down my back. Soon I greet the twilight.

Chapter 11
Lucian

I take in the woman resting on my thigh. An electric current sings through my blood, starting a steady hum in my ears. Her left hand has unfurled, palm laying directly above my knee, creating a pocket of warmth. Gently, I brush stray strands of hair away from her face with the pads of my fingers. The cut from our first encounter has started to heal, though she needs to put more salve on it to stave off infection. Her breathing has evened out and I take my time looking my fill without the fear of being caught.

I can only see half of her face but that doesn't take away from her beauty. Full, light pink lips hang slightly open in slumber. Brown eyelashes lay against a pale freckled cheek and her long hair has started to come unbound from the plait she's had it in since yesterday. The blue dress she wears is covered in dust and dirt, but she hasn't seemed to mind. A modest, square neckline reveals more of her pale skin and hints at the curves hidden beneath.

I recall how she looked in the candlelight with nothing on but her shift and suppress a groan. A vision she was, an angel sent to chase away my demons. She has a few scars decorating her skin, and I wonder how she got them.

She looks so fragile the way she is curled into herself, but she has the build of a fighter. Leggings outlined strong legs during our ride, and she certainly knows her way around a saddle.

I can see the shape of the dagger stashed in her pocket, and I know we will need to find her a proper belt to carry the weapon. There may even be one in this basement somewhere, I make a mental note to rummage for one in the morning.

Grabbing her removed cloak, I drape it over her to keep her warm. In sleep the worry lines around her eyes have disappeared, and she looks at peace for the first time since I met her. Hopefully, the Shadows do not find her this eve.

"I've seen that look before," comes a hushed voice to my right. Samson is watching me in the low light while he sharpens a knife. Not a Seraphim blade but one of the others hidden on his person.

"What look is that?" I ask softly, glancing at Flor to make sure I haven't woken her.

"The look of a man who is smitten," Samson grins down at his task.

"I am just trying to offer some comfort. The last few days haven't been the easiest, and she has faced each new revelation with an incredible amount of bravery. If anything, I admire her courage and willingness to try to understand a world she knows nothing about." I tighten my grip around her.

"Sure lad, wha'ever ye say," he chuckles and continues running a whetstone over his blade.

I mull over his words and agree that maybe I am a bit taken by her. How could I not be, though even if I've only known her for a short amount of time? She isn't just beautiful on the outside but possesses a great inner light as well. She is stubborn and witty, but also compassionate and resourceful. Her willingness to express her doubts and show her genuine emotions is commendable when it would seem most people hide behind false sentiments.

Tracing a small scar on her collarbone, Samson speaks again, "Those marks ye see are self-inflicted. Tha dreams would get so bad, she'd unintentionally hurt herself, claw at her skin to wake up."

My admiration for her continues to grow. Such trauma she has endured yet remains untouched by it, not letting it jade her.

A barely audible clicking sound causes me to still my fingers and lift my head. Samson is already on his feet facing the door leading to the tunnels, weapon held in front of him. I see Thierry motion for Gregg to wake Aric and Aggie. Wallace holds a short sword and has flanked Samson.

Gently, I shake Florence. Her eyes pop open, and I hold a finger to her lips to keep her from speaking, tiny pinpricks of energy sizzling underneath my skin. Wild gaze searching mine, she slowly sits up. Blinking groggily at Samson and Wallace, she removes the dagger from her pocket, unsheathing the blade, she focuses her gaze.

The clicking of the door's latch has stopped and we wait. I am on my feet standing directly in front of Flor with a short, curved blade from Namid in hand. I hear the rustle of her clothes as she fidgets behind me. My pulse thrums steadily through my veins, and I count the beats.

One.

Two.

Three.

Finally, the door slowly rotates outward, inch by agonizing inch. I crouch into a fighting stance, ready to defend our small hideout. The glare from a lantern blinds us when the door completely opens. I can only make out the silhouette of a rather large person behind it.

"Donna move, or it will be tha las' thing ye do," growls Samson.

The newcomer freezes, and Thierry takes over. He instructs, "Slowly put down the lantern and any weapon you may have. Walk into the room where we can see your face."

Placing the lantern on the ground, the visitor walks into the dimly-lit basement with hands raised and a hood covering his head. I immediately recognize him from the inn where we stopped the day before last. Dark green cloak with a pattern of knots sewn in gold thread around the edges.

"That's far enough," says Thierry. "Remove your hood."

The stranger removes his hood and an audible gasp can be heard around the room.

"It canna be."

"No shite."

"I must be seeing things."

"Back from the dead."

"Athair?" I spin and look at Florence who has dropped her dagger and is staring at the man in the doorway. I turn back around and instantly identify the intruder, William Stuart, Florence's father. His presence has always demanded attention, and the years have done little to change that. Hair the same shade as his daughter's is tied away from a face that is half covered in a shaggy salt-and-pepper beard. His nose looks like it has been broken once or twice and tired brown eyes linger on Florence.

"Will?" Samson sounds dumbfounded. Recovering, he pulls William into a rough hug. "How in tha Three Kingdoms is it possible tha' no' one but two dead men return from tha grave simultaneously?"

"It is good to see you too, Samson," he says returning his friend's embrace. Stepping back, William locks eyes with Florence over my shoulder. "Flossy."

Letting out a choked sob, Florence speaks, "Is it really you?"

"Aye, it is me, pet. I am so sorry I've been away for so long."

"I-I thought you were dead. We all did. How is this possible?" She asks, bewildered. "I watched the bridge collapse. I watched as you were swept downriver. We looked for you for days." She says, walking around me to get a better look. I lower my blade but don't put it away, I want to be sure this man is who he says he is. It's been a decade since I've seen him, and five for Florence. Memory can be a tricky thing. Your mind can fill in the gaps with false information especially if there is hope for a happy ending.

"Five years ago, our worst nightmare came to pass, and our small oasis was discovered," he explains. "We fought like hell to keep you safe, but the Reapers were too much for us to handle on our own. We've never fought more than one at a time. Usually, they work alone but those three were well organized and fought as a unit. Once we realized it was a planned attack, it was too late. We walked right into their trap. Your mother and I managed to slay two of them but the third got across the river before the bridge collapsed." He reaches a hand out, but Florence backs up a step. Lowering it he asks, "What do you remember of that night, Flossy?"

"All I remember is waking up next to the river and watching you both plunge into the water, never to be seen again."

"Do you remember how you got there?" William asks softly.

"Samson told me I was sleepwalking. When you realized I was gone, I had already made it to the center of the old bridge. I don't remember what I was dreaming about, but I'd never done that before," a look of guilt colors her features. "But you still haven't answered how you survived. And where have you been this whole time?"

I can tell Florence is still weary of the newcomer and needs confirmation that this man is her father. Smart girl.

"I was swept down river along with your mother. The current was quick, but the river becomes a little shallower as you approach Wolfewater. I grabbed hold of Laila and kept us a float. I don't know how long we rode the current before I hauled us both to shore. Her wounds were extensive. She was bleeding out through a jagged gash in her side, bestowed on her by the Reaper she killed. I tried to staunch the flow, but she had already lost too much blood. Her lips were blue, and she couldn't keep her eyes open. That was when I knew she wouldn't make it. The water was too cold, I couldn't get her warm. I held her close as she left this world. She died in my arms." William pauses and inhales a shaky breath.

"Laila used her last breath to make sure you were safe, Florence, she gave the last of her energy to save you. I buried her in an unmarked grave next to the water, letting her return to the earth. The river swept us most of the way to Wolfewater. A man there owed me a debt, so I borrowed a horse and went in search of Kalligan, knowing Samson would keep you safe. We realized that the three had come through the Darkwell gate virtually undetected. We sealed it for good. I didn't mean to leave you Florence, I didn't. My need to track down the third Reaper overrode every other instinct, and I became obsessed with its end. The hunt became my reason for breathing. I couldn't bear to face you with that monster still being alive when your mother wasn't.

"I searched for years. It would jump in and out of the Shadows, and I'd lose the trail. Five long years passed, and I realized I had abandoned everything I loved. It was no longer about keeping you safe, it was about vengeance. I had neglected my duties as a father.

"What you must think of me. I let you believe I was dead, so I could satisfy my selfish need for retribution instead of coming home to mourn the loss of your mother. I should've been there to help you pick up the pieces, and instead, I left you alone. I am so sorry.

"I was on my way home to beg your forgiveness when the Reaper I had been tracking materialized outside Grimsfield." William turns to address Samson, "Laila crafted a barrier around the village as her last act on this plane. Somehow, it has fallen. Something broke through her shield."

"Shite," is Samson's only reply to that cryptic statement.

"The Reaper shouldn't have been able to enter the village, but it did. It had fled by the time I made it to the shop. I tried to find you, but you weren't there, Florence. The back door was open, and I assumed you stepped out, soon to return. I wanted to see if I could track the creature. I dug out my dagger from the hidden compartment in the drawer and hastily wrote you a note telling you I'd be back once all was quiet. I was hoping you'd recognize the handwriting and that the Reaper hadn't found you. The dagger serving as my signature because I didn't want to alert anyone else I had returned, in case someone else found the note before you."

"I did not know who the note was from, aither. You're supposed to be dead. I wouldn't have thought it was from you. And the Reaper found me. It came in through the front door, and I ran out the back. It pulled me into the Shadow Territories, which by the way, I know now what that is," her brow puckering in agitation. "Lucian brought me back," she gives me a grateful look over her shoulder. Confused she adds, "What do you mean mathiar saved me with her last breath? And what barrier are you talking about?"

Thierry rubs his hands together and says, "Looks like we won't be getting any more sleep tonight. Shut the door William and come have a seat. It would seem you've got some explaining to do." Pulling the door closed, William takes a seat close to Florence and waves to the space beside him. She gives me one last look and sits down next to her father.

"It's time for you to learn who you are Flossy."

Chapter 12
Florence

"Who I am?" I ask, continuing to glance at Lucian like he might have answers. He has become my rock in this free fall I've found myself in. I look back at the living ghost next to me, hoping he can make sense of this mess.

"Thinking back on everything that has happened, I think your mother and I may have made a mistake keeping you so sheltered. We hoped that by removing ourselves from this world and allowing you to remain ignorant of our past and your heritage, it would somehow keep you out of harm's way. So, before I begin, just know I love you deeply Flossy. As did your mother. I've made a lot of mistakes in my life, but making you was not one of them."

I can feel my palms start to sweat while nerves light sparks under my skin. My father is sitting next to me in this dark, dank basement below a city full of death. He is watching me with eyes full of regret and sadness. Anticipation rips through my body, and my need for answers overrides any hesitation I might have. "I love you too, aither. But this has been a lot to process, and I still cannot believe you are real-and here. Whatever you have to tell me won't be as bad as walking through a ransacked city, shrouded in death and ash."

William sags with relief. Everyone else has taken seats around us so they too can hear what my father has to say. Aric and Aggie have lit a few more candles and are now passing around a bag of dried berries. Wallace and Gregg sharpen blades while Thierry lounges on his pile of blankets. Samson and Lucian both look extremely tense but for different reasons.

Lucian still eyes my father with suspicion and has edged closer to where we are sitting. Samson seems nervous, like William will produce a Reaper out of his pocket.

Drawing in a fortifying breath he begins, "Let's get it all out there, shall we? Your mother isn't from the Highlands of Rolum like Samson and I are. That was a lie we told you to keep your past hidden."

At least he has the decency to look ashamed, I think. "Then where was she from?" I sound a little patronizing, but who wouldn't?

"Laila hails from the Isiwen capital, Ryntaesi. Her father was a blacksmith, the best blacksmith in all Three Kingdoms. People from every corner of this land would travel to Ryntaesi to have Connak craft them a blade. Kalligan, Samson and I traveled there one summer because we heard that Connak was experimenting with the Fae metal, Atrum. It was rumored that this metal could kill Reapers almost instantly. The magic from the Living Forest is an intrinsic part of the metal and works against the dark magic of the Shadows and the Reapers. We wanted to see if the rumors were true," he says shrugging his shoulders. "I met her while we were working with Connak to craft a new kind of Seraphim Blade, the dagger you carry was one of the first created." I touch it through the fabric of my skirt, and his eyes follow the movement. I want to ask what happened to my mother's blade, but he continues before I can.

"Your mother, her mother and her mother before her, as well as all the women in their line were what we would call mystics or witches. But among the people of Isiwen, they were known as Fae. Your mother was a Fae healer, Florence. Basically, what all this means, is you are half Fae," he smirks. "As she died, she used the last of her energy to create a barrier around Grimsfield to keep the Reapers out. She put her soul into that spell and sealed off the village from any Fae threat, dark or otherwise."

"That must've been why the dreams stopped," I muse but immediately remember what he said about my mother being Fae. "Me? I am half Fae? I thought Fae were supposed to be beautiful and flawless? I mean maither was beautiful, almost painfully so. But you have seen me, right?" I blurt these thoughts, gesturing to myself. "I am just a regular girl, there is nothing special about me."

"You do not see the way those around you see you," he says, poking me in the chest.

"I guess," I utter. "But what does this mean?"

"It means yer a rare breed, lass," Samson interjects, looking like he might bolt.

"You are a Halfling, Flossy. And you should not exist."

"Not exist..." I am dumbfounded.

"It is difficult for Humans and Fae to conceive, it is uncommon but does happen. When it occurs, the resulting offspring are executed immediately after birth. Halflings can be dangerous creatures. Many years ago, a boy, just like you, opened the first rift between the Shadow Territories and our world. Because you are half human and half Fae-neither one nor the other-you become a funnel for energy or magic, both light and dark. The boy began feeding off dark magic, craving it. It gave him enough power to equal a full-blooded Fae. One day, he took too much and created a hole into the

Shadows. That hole was here in Darkwell. The first Reapers came through and seized control of the boy, overloading his system, using him to create other pathways across the Kingdoms. He was discarded after he served his purpose.

"This was the start of the War of Light. For eight years, humans and Fae fought the Reapers side by side, eventually pushing them back into the Shadows and regaining control of the gateways. Because the original creator was gone, they could not close the fractures fully, and the council of the Three Kingdoms created the Seraphim Order. An inter-kingdom and inter-race group trained specifically to police the gates and monitor Reaper activity. We let them shepherd the dying onto the next life. They are still able to feed off those souls, but they are ready to cross into the next life, into the Shadow Territories and offer little in the way of heightened strength.

"However, during the war, almost all the Halflings were persecuted and put to death by the people in their own towns. They were held accountable for the actions of one misguided boy. Those who managed to survive the culling went into hiding and lived out their days anonymously. The Fae court in Isiwen decreed that any Halfling created from that day forward would not draw a first breath. The Kingdoms of Rolum and Namid agreed, and so, half-breeds became illegal," he concludes, laying his hand over my clenched fists.

Lucian's eyes light with something akin to wonder as he says, "You're a Conduit, Flor. You can call upon energy from the Shadows and from the Living Forest. Since you do not have magic inherent within you like the Fae do, you draw it from the world around you."

"Your mother and I did not want to lose you, so we left the Order to raise you. The only people who knew of your existence were Kalligan and Samson," nodding in the other man's direction. "They swore to protect our secret and to protect you."

"We set up our new life in Grimsfield and tried to distance ourselves from the Fae, the Reapers and the Order to build a normal life," he tightens his lips and squeezes my hands. "Your night terrors are glimpses into the Shadow Territories, pet. We were not always able to shield you in sleep, and dark magic always finds a way in. The tea we would give you when you woke was brewed by your mother to help remove your memories of that horrible place. We didn't want to expose you to the world we left or let your existence be discovered by the people who would kill you simply for being born."

Lucian strides over and lays a reassuring hand on my shoulder, offering comfort. He looks almost sad when I finally meet his gaze.

"You hid this from me and let me believe there was something wrong with me," anger burns through my voice. "The other kids shunned me, aither."

"But isn't that better than being dead? You had a family who loved you and you grew up without the fear of being hunted by your own people. Does that not count for something?" He pleads.

"You could've told me. We could've hidden the secret together, and I would have finally had an explanation for why I would wake up, crippled by fear, unable to remember what had happened." I stand up to move away from this man I thought I knew. Lucian backs up to give me space, like he knows I need to work out my anxiety.

I can barely process everything I have learned. I've been blindsided by the one person I trusted fully in this life. First, discovering that he was alive and well, then uncovering the truth of my dreams. I understand, but that doesn't lessen the betrayal. I feel like I have been robbed of some essential part of me. The part that would understand this panic and tenuous hold I have on sanity.

"I need air." Storming toward the door I demand, "Let me out!" I stare at the space where the secret passage will open, waiting for someone to oblige. A hand reaches around me, catches the latch and pushes the door outward.

"Take the tunnel to the right. You will find a ladder that leads to the courtyard of the Keep. Stay hidden," Thierry appears on my periphery.

"I'll go with you, just in case," Lucian offers.

I jerk my head to the door and step into the stillness of the sewers.

Chapter 13
Lucian

Following Flor out into the tunnels puts me on edge. We aren't sure what is left within the city or within the Keep. The relative safety of the courtyard should be a fine place to enjoy fresh air, but I do not wish to linger. Who knows what has been unearthed in the night. The gateway is unguarded, and opportunistic survivors may be looting the remnants of the city. She is several paces ahead of me walking briskly, shoulders tense, hands still curled into tight fists. I don't dare speak until we reach the surface.

Climbing up the ladder, there appears to be a trap door leading into the courtyard. Florence reaches up and pushes the door high enough that she can see out, checking if the coast is clear. It must seem safe, because she raises it the rest of the way, laying it on the ground. Hiking up her skirt, she places one knee on the ground and hoists herself out. Poking my head out of the top, Florence waits for me a few meters away. I pull myself out and dust off my pants, leaving the door open in case we need to make a hasty retreat.

I'm barely a step away from the hatch when she flings angry words at me, voice rising into the night. "How could he do this? Let me think he was dead, scare me half to death with a mysterious note, then return only to tell me most of my life was a lie!"

"Lower your voice, Flor, we don't know what is beyond these walls," I coax, placating. "You have a right to be upset, your life has changed a staggering amount in a very short period of time. But you also must see the reason behind the deception. He only wanted a life for you. A life away from all this," I sweep my arms out to encompass the entirety of the Keep.

Neither of us look up at Kalligan's still suspended body, but she knows what I mean. Some of the fire leaves her eyes as she takes in the surrounding destruction. The Keep, as formidable as it is, wasn't impermeable to the flames or death. The courtyard is an enclosed space off the dining hall where a body lies halfway out of the doorway, feet pointing in odd directions, congealed blood a dark stain haloing the corpse. The ground is littered with ash and the grass next to the trap door is nothing but soot.

A vegetable garden grew close to the kitchen door and where there used to be several tables with benches, a pile of broken and charred remains. The Reapers destroyed everything they could. The annihilation of the city was swift and complete.

Tragedy hangs in the air like a mournful sigh. This place may never be rebuilt.

"He hurt me, Lucian. The image I had memorialized of my father will be forever tainted by this new, deceitful version. He should've stayed away." Crossing her arms over her chest, something she does when she is feeling exposed I've noticed, cuffs her shoes in the dirt.

"If he would've stayed away, you may never have known what you are. You now have an explanation for your night terrors and why you saw Kalligan's death. You can use this knowledge Florence, to try to understand what powers you have, to fight back. Little is known of Conduits anymore after the mass purge. You could be the key to finally closing the gates for good." I, too, have a secret I've been keeping from her. Knowing that she is a Halfling Conduit has clicked several clues into place, but I must ease into it. She is still raw from her father's admission, and I'm not sure now is the best time to add to the fire. "What if I help you figure out the extent of your power? I can teach you how to handle a blade, to defend yourself if you find your way into the Shadows again."

The last bit does the trick. I can tell she is letting some of the anger go in favor of finding a purpose.

"I can handle a blade Lucian. I already told you, you caught me by surprise, that is why you disarmed me so easily," she says self-consciously.

"Of course. We will just give you a refresher, get you used to using a Seraphim Blade. I can teach you all the best places to strike a Reaper. And I'm sure you can show me a thing or two as well," winking, for some reason I can't help but goad her.

"You might be surprised at my talent," she baits, confident. "My father was an excellent teacher," sadness clouds her face again. "Let's talk about something else. What were your parents like?" She asks as she looks up at the still dark sky.

The stars are bright against the deep of the night when the city lights aren't washing out the splendor. Dawn will soon be upon us. The moon has set, and the Keep sits higher than the rest of the city. I can see that the horizon is lighter out over the water of the bay. The courtyard offers a beautiful view across the Klelk Sea.

"I didn't really know my parents," I say, watching the skyline. "I was so close with my cousin because my aunt and uncle raised me like I was their own son. My parents liked to gamble, and when their debts became too high, dropped me at Niall's house and never looked back."

"How old were you?"

"I was five when they said their goodbyes. I didn't know it at the time, but that was the last I ever saw of them. They were never around much anyway, and I was welcomed with open arms by my cousin's family-so I never really missed them."

A sad smile plays on her lips, "Then I am glad you had them. Have you seen your aunt or uncle since you have returned?"

At this, I look away, her father and I have more in common than she might think. "I have not been to see them in my time back on this plane. I understand William when he says he did not want to face you when he could not avenge your mother. I'm afraid they won't want to see me and remind them that their son is never coming back."

"But you killed the Reaper who stole Niall's soul. You were trapped because of your love for him."

"It was my idea to try to face the Reaper to begin with. I am responsible for his death." Admitting it out loud claws deep furrows of shame within me.

"You were young, and you both knew the risks when you joined the Order, so did your aunt and uncle. You cannot blame yourself forever, Lucian. Niall would not want it. He made his own choices, same as you," placing a hand on the side of my face she lowers my chin so that I am looking at her. "Forgive yourself. You did your penance in the Shadows. Your Aunt and Uncle will want to know you are alive. I see that now. I would rather know that my father is still breathing than go on thinking he isn't, even if he has been absent for five years. They will forgive you just like I will forgive my father." Giving me a reassuring nod, she caresses my cheek and then drops her hand. "I guess we should head back down before they come looking for us. Most of my anger has subsided, and I think I need to apologize for my abrupt exit."

I grab her arm to keep her from turning away, "Thank you, Florence." A grin spreads across her face, and she is about to say something when her eyes become unfocused.

Her smile wilts, and her voice is barely a whisper when she finally speaks, "We are not alone."

Chapter 14
Florence

My eyes refocus as Lucian's start to shine. I know what's about to happen.

"Your eyes, they are glowing," I tell him, stepping back to draw my blade out of my pocket.

Black smudges fly past my head, the cold descending. "I felt the ripple behind me," he says in a hushed voice. "Can you see it?" Leaning to the side, I squint around him. A shadow detaches itself from the wall beside the kitchen door. I point with my blade and Lucian twists to face the oncoming threat, pulling duel curved knives from his waist.

The colors around us have muted, but I can see twin orbs of crimson beneath the Reaper's hood. He looks similar to the one I encountered but is smaller in stature. The cloak hides its upper half, while leather breaches are tucked into shin-high black boots. Nothing can be seen inside the hood besides its eyes. I wonder what its head looks like. Gloved hands tighten around twin axes, and I gulp in deep drags of air. A low rumble emanates from the direction of the creature, and a second shadow slinks out of the darkness.

"I see you brought a friend," Lucian directs at the shadows. "I need you to stay behind me Flor, get to the trap door if you can. I don't want to put those alleged skills to the test."

"Easier said than done," I manage past the lump in my throat. The beasts stand on the other side of our escape. We should've closed the door. It knows we were hiding in the tunnels.

Lucian echoes my thoughts, "We have to kill them, or the hideout will be compromised. If you have to, find an opening to get a strike in with the Seraphim Blade, the metal will do the rest. Otherwise, try to make it underground. I'll work to take out the wolf first, I've dealt with plenty of their kind."

Not wasting any time, he gives me a nod and rushes at the Lyall with unearthly speed. I realize then what Lucian meant when he said the Shadows can change a person. Beside his glowing eyes, he has gained speed more common among the Fae, if I remember the legends correctly. I am no longer convinced he is completely human as I watch his movements blur.

I track the Reaper's movements, keeping an eye on Lucian and the massive wolf.

Snapping jaws barely miss his arm as Lucian swipes at the Lyall's muzzle with one of his curved blades. Standing at eye level with the beast, the wolf bares two rows of dripping teeth and bows to launch in his direction again.

Finding the Reaper has snuck around the outside trying to get at Lucian's backside, I shout, "Watch your back!"

I go unheard as he and wolf circle around one another. I swivel to face the new threat fully, preparing to engage and hoping like hell I can still handle a dagger. After my parents disappeared, I stopped training. I couldn't bring myself to look at my father's blade anymore, the fight dying within me. Sending up a quick prayer to anyone listening, I shake off five years of stagnation. Squeezing the jeweled hilt, I move my feet into a proper fighting stance.

"Hey! Ugly! Over here." The Reaper whips its head in my direction, and a great puff of air coalesces around its body. "Can't take that back now, Florence," I tell myself tensing my arm muscles, setting my feet.

We square off, and a voice wraps itself around my cerebrum and vibrates through my core; the Reaper is speaking. "Ah, the hidden Halfling. I'll enjoy your tasting your soul."

"Don't let him rattle you, don't let him rattle you," I chant. "Well then, come and get it," I yell to the creature. I can still see Lucian and the wolf, locked in their morbid dance. Hopefully, this buys him enough time to slay the Lyall.

Mirroring the Reapers movements, years of training roll through my brain. "There it is," I sneer, confidence building as muscle memory takes over. It faints to my left and I jolt to cover my weak side. Falling back, he does the same to my right, toying with me.

I've had about enough of that.

I spring into action, lunging with my blade arm toward his chest. The Reaper goes to block with an ax, and I spin to my right, throwing him off balance. If I had another weapon, I would've been able to land a blow with my left arm. Following me around, I can feel the breeze of the ax in his right hand as it whizzes past my shoulder. Completing my spin, we face off again.

He moves first this time, swinging at me with both arms, one after another. I have to retreat but keep my blade raised. Side-swiping at my head, I duck and manage to stab upward toward his arm, slicing through the sleeve. Unfortunately, I didn't find the skin beneath.

A loud whine rents the air, and we both turn to see Lucian pull twin blades from the wolf's neck. Head lulling, the Lyall slumps to the ground. Blood pools beneath a lifeless body before it begins to steam and evaporate back into the Shadows. Flicking the blood from his Namidian scimitars, Lucian falls in beside me.

Leveling an ax at each of us, the Reaper advances. I move first, blocking a blown from the left side. The hit sending a jolt of pain through my arm. I make it inside his guard and bury my blade in his shoulder.

I stumble backward and skid out of range. Light floods from the wound, and Lucian follows through, removing the creature's head. I cover my ears as a high-pitched screech accompanies the collapse of the Reaper. All that is left is a pile of smoking clothes and my dagger, lying atop the cloak.

Immediately the world rights itself. Colors return, and the night is crisp but no longer freezing.

"I stand corrected," Lucian's says while he wipes the blood from his swords.

"Apology accepted." I walk over to the still smoking cloak and pluck my dagger from the folds. "Did you see the light?" I ask amazed.

"That is what happens when Seraphim Blades made of Atrum strike a being from the Shadows. The light magic negates the dark, spreading, snuffing it out." Tucking the scimitars back into his belt he walks over. "You did well Flor."

The approval blooms in my chest and heats my cheeks, "You didn't do so bad yourself," I say deflecting the compliment. "It pulled us into the Shadows again. Is it because the gate has been reopened?"

"It is because you are a Conduit, Florence. The Reapers can use the energy constantly flooding your body to pull you into the Shadows, creating a new gate. That is why you are so dangerous. You receive both light and dark magic equally.

It just depends on which flow you want to tap into," he explains. Turning to me, he runs a hand through his hair, "I need to tell you something Flor..." but he is interrupted by Samson poking his head out of the trap door.

"Oy, what happened here? Heard a lot a screamin' and bangin'."

"We were ambushed. A Reaper and a Lyall pulled us into the Shadows and tried to kill us," I tell Samson as he hefts his weight out of the hole.

"Looks like ye took care of 'em." Samson kicks at the crumbled robes and looks at the puddle of blood the Lyall left.

"More will come," says Lucian, ever practical. "We need to round up the remaining survivors as soon as we can and get them out of the city."

"Let's go below and report ta tha others. Thierry will want ta know what's happened. Aric and Aggie can lead us ta the others," replies Samson, ambling back to the ladder.

"What were you going to tell me Lucian?" I ask, Halting his escape back to the tunnels.

"Next time we are alone, Flor." With a flutter of his cloak he descends back to the sewers.

Chapter 15
Florence

Aric, Aggie, Wallace and Gregg are hounding Lucian for details of the fight like school children.

"How big was the wolf?"

"Did you sever the head clean?"

"I remember my first battle, bout shit myself."

"Where did Florence hit it?"

"You made it out unharmed?"

"Have you seen that Reaper before?"

The questions are endless, and Lucian looks uncomfortable with all the attention. His spots me over their heads and throws me a pleading look. Laughing, I look back at my father, Samson and Thierry who don't look as amused.

"Tell us again what happened, Flossy."

"We were in the courtyard talking when I felt the air get colder and all the colors vanished. Lucian's eyes began to glow blue, and I saw black spots out of the corner of my eyes, the same thing that happened a few days ago. The Reaper and the Lyall came out of the shadows by the kitchen door, and we fought them. We won," I say sitting up a little straighter. Proud of myself for not running and remembering my training.

Thierry sits with his arms folded, while Samson and my father share a look. I can't decipher what it means, but I don't think it is good.

"I am so glad you are safe, pet," my father says, pulling me into a rough hug and then releasing me like he forgot I was angry with him. "I know I upset you, but we shouldn't have let you leave. I just got you back and I can't lose you now."

"It is ok, aither. I am fine, and I remembered everything you taught me," I say beaming.

He returns my smile, "you always were a little force with a blade."

Deflating a little, I admit, "I am sorry for storming away like that, I may have overreacted. All that information was a lot to process." Shrugging one shoulder I look at him from beneath my lashes.

"I'm sorry too, Flossy. For everything. If I could take it all back, I would, and maybe you would've been more prepared for all of this. More prepared to defend yourself. I just worry about you."

"I held my own, and Lucian was with me. We handled the situation," I sound like I am whining, and maybe I am. I've kept myself alive for five years without his help, he doesn't have to start worrying now.

"I know, I know, but I am still your father..."

"I know, aither." Laying my head on his shoulder, I hope the contact will let him know I'm on my way to forgiving him.

We are all silent for a moment when Samson starts, "About Lucian, lass-"

"What about him?" I ask defensively, cutting him off.

"You said his eyes were glowing. Did this happen while you were in the Shadows?" My father continues, I can feel the rumble of his voice in my cheek.

"Yes, they were like that the day I met him as well, when he brought me back," I say lifting my head.

"We think he might not be entirely human anymore, Flossy. And that worries us."

"That worries all of you, or just you, aither?" He seems to have picked up on my growing attachment to Lucian. But I had the same thought myself and it never occurred to me to be afraid of him, well not after I learned who he was.

"Mostly me. But I think we need to be careful here. I suspect he has somehow absorbed the properties of the Shadows. That makes him dangerous." He holds up a hand to stop my reply. "Samson was filling me in on everything that has happened while you two were outside. Your mother and I may have retired, but we weren't ignorant to what was happening. I've met Lucian a handful of times when I'd travel to Darkwell, and he has changed. We also knew of his disappearance, and I was shocked to see him standing in this basement with you. I just want you to be cautious."

"But aren't I dangerous too? What if we just ask him, I'm sure he can explain everything?" I start to call him over when Samson touches my arm.

"We just don't want ye ta get attached lass, in case somethin' were ta happen," he flicks his eyes to where Lucian is still fending off questions.

"Are you saying you think he will betray us?"

"I'm just saying anythin' is possible," and he lets me go.

Mulling over that unsettling turn in the conversation, I walk over to the other group and wedge myself between Lucian and his admirers. "Alright, give it a rest everybody. I think he's answered enough questions for today. It's not like you've never encountered a Reaper before," I scold.

"We know, but we've never met someone who has made it out of the Shadows before to tell the tale, let alone fought off a Reaper and a Lyall on their own." Aggie says, appraising Lucian. She is beautiful, in the traditional way of the Fae. Tall and lean, with a perfectly symmetrical face, violet eyes and blonde hair falling down her back. Her skin glows in the candlelight, and I must admit she is lovely. Her brother, Aric, looks like the male version but with sharper features. Where she is soft and feminine, he is all harsh lines. His jawline could have been cut from granite, and his high cheekbones give him a regal air. He, too, is lovely. I remember Thierry said they were twins from Isiwen, the homeland of most Fae.

"I was there too, you know. Even got in a shot before Lucian beheaded the monster." Heavens, I sound like a child. But, I don't like being dismissed and I definitely don't like the way her eyes linger on Lucian's face.

I slap myself internally and cut that thought off at the knees. I have no reason to be worrying about whose eyes are lingering on whom. We only just met and who knows what is going to happen in the coming days. We are just building a friendship and nothing else. I have other things I should be worrying about anyway, like being a funnel for light and dark magic. I don't have time to get attached to a particularly handsome mystery of a man.

And there I go again.

Aggie is giving me a look down her nose as Lucian extracts us from the conversation, "She is right. She was there and held her own like a real hunter. Don't you guys need to strategize about how we are going to move the civilians in a few hours?" He nods to the twins.

Rolling her eyes, she motions for her brother to follow, "Let's go Aric. I don't feel like ruffling any more feathers." The pair walks back to the map and I can feel heat crawling up my neck. It is one thing to be jealous, it is another to be called on it. Wallace mumbles something about a spoil sport and Gregg smacks him on the back of the head. Now I am officially embarrassed.

"Thank you for saving me," Lucian says. "They wouldn't stop asking questions. I'm not used to being the center of attention anymore." He's not looking at me while he is talking, and that makes me feel even worse. Of course, he wouldn't understand this weird sense of loyalty I have to him. I'm not the one who has saved his life multiple times. One more reason to lock down any stray thoughts of Lucian and his lips.

Another internal slap.

"Would you like to tell me whatever you were going to tell me before Samson came looking for us?" I ask, steering the conversation to a safer place. I want to give him the opportunity to explain himself before I address my father's concerns.

He still has yet to look at me and is fidgeting with the cuffs of the jacket he wears under his cloak, which he has yet to remove. It is a very boyish gesture. He may look like a man, but I guess when you reach adulthood alone inside a living nightmare, some traits aren't so easily lost.

I am about to ask again when he pierces me with a vulnerable look, "I'm sure you have noticed that there are things about me that are strange. You commented on my eyes but that isn't the only thing." I wait for him to continue, afraid he might stop.

"I am able to move at close to Fae speeds and although I have been eating in front of you, I do not have to eat to stay alive." The last part surprises me. I watched him fight so I know he can move incredibly quick but to be able to exist without food gives me pause.

"I watched you battle the Lyall, so I know of your speed and your eyes glow only when you are in the Shadows, but how can you exist without eating?" I try not to let my hesitation show as I think about what Samson said.

"I don't want to frighten you Florence, but I need to be honest with you." He doesn't wait for a response before hurrying on, "I am not sure exactly when it happened but being in the Shadows for so long has made me more like the Reapers. My eyes have adjusted, so I can see beyond the veil when I'm in the Territories. That is why they glow. My body can now move at speeds close to the things that dwell there, and I do not need to eat human food. I still enjoy the taste, but it is not necessary for life. The magic of the Shadows found a way into my body and keeps me alive. You could say I am a halfling now too," he gives me a halfhearted smile. "I've become part Reaper and can only survive close to a source of dark magic."

"How did you figure all this out?" I ask, genuinely curious now.

"I first discovered that dark magic was becoming a part of me when I was going through practice maneuvers with my Seraphim Blade, to keep myself fresh while trying to find my way out of the Shadows. I got clumsy and nicked my hand. Instead of bleeding, the cut released light. I thought that was going to be my end, but the wound knit itself back together. I guess the metal didn't completely destroy me, because I'm still part human."

"Interesting, and the food..."

"The moment I returned, I relieved a gentleman of his coin purse and headed for the first inn I could. I ordered three bowls of stew and ate them all. But I was still hungry. I didn't want to waste all the coin, so I decided to wait and see what would happen. I became distracted by trying to track the Reaper I had followed through, and I didn't think about food for a while. I traveled to the next closest gate, assuming the Reaper would need to go back through to regain its strength. I stopped at an inn close to the portal for the night. I was too exhausted to eat, so I went to my room to sleep. When I woke up, I felt a tingling sensation throughout my whole body. I looked down at my hands. They were becoming translucent. That's when I felt a ripple and a pull to the gateway. Panicking, I went to the rift and attempted to jump through. I made it with ease. Immediately I became whole, and my hunger subsided. That's when I realized the dark magic of the Shadows sustained me, and I could've found my way back at any time. Once back on our side, I didn't want others to catch on and would eat when others would eat and return to the Territories long enough to recharge. I learned I could feel when something would go in and out of the Shadows close to me and tracked the Reaper that way."

I am silent for a moment, deciding most of this is possible. "You know you shouldn't steal, Lucian. I could have you arrested," I can tell this was not what he expected me to say and laughs. He has a wonderful laugh.

"You always find the most miniscule facts to latch on to. Me stealing can't be the only part of that you heard," he says lifting a brow.

"No, but I deal with stress in odd ways," waving my hand in the air to dismiss the topic. "How long can you be here before you have to go back?"

"This is what I wanted to talk to you about. I can be outside of the Shadows for about twelve hours before I feel the pull to return."

"Between our first meeting and now you've been away longer than twelve hours, Lucian," I say, trying to piece everything together.

"Exactly. Usually at about hour six, I will start to feel a tingle in my limbs, but not when I'm around you. I have been decidedly whole since I met you." Tentatively he touches my cheek and it's like I've touched lightning. Something within me bubbles to the surface, seeking where his fingers touch. "See."

"But I've touched your skin before, and this didn't happen," I say alarmed.

"I wasn't actively seeking your energy when you touched me then, I shut down my need for it. I didn't want to scare you. At most, you felt a slight pulse." I think about all the time we have made contact, and the energy that seemed to race under my skin. It was never unpleasant. In fact, it was enjoyable.

"Whoa, ok. So, what does this mean for us?"

"Bare bones of it? You are keeping me alive, Flor."

Chapter 16
Lucian

I watch Florence try to work through everything I have just said. Two creases form between her brows, and I can practically hear the wheels turning in her head.

"Let me make sure I understand you correctly, I, Florence Stuart," pointing to her chest then pointing at mine, "am keeping you, Lucian Campbell, alive because I am a Halfling Conduit, and you are some sort of hybrid Reaper-human. Does that cover it?"

"Yes, that covers it, though you put it more eloquently than I did."

"I wasn't sure things could get any weirder, and yet, here we are," she lets out a nervous chuckle. "I don't understand any of this, but it seems you're going to be stuck with me if you don't want to return to the Shadows. And for that, I am sorry."

"I happen to enjoy your company, I am not in the least bit sorry." An endearing blush creeps up from her neckline, and she looks away. Flattery makes her uncomfortable, and I tuck that information away for later use.

Clearing my throat, I tear my eyes from her neck, now blushing myself.

"Samson and my father suspect you are part Shadow and have some worries concerning your new," rolling her wrist searching for word, "abilities," she finishes.

"Then let's go put their minds at ease, hmm?" On our way back to Samson and William, I take in the rest of our troop. The twins are briefing Wallace, Gregg and Thierry on the whereabouts of the survivors and discussing the best way to mobilize them. The two men in question seem to be in the middle of a heated argument when we approach. Once we are within earshot, they immediately drop whatever they were talking about.

"Aither, I think you need to hear what Lucian has to say," she says, stepping out of the way for me to address them.

I give them a more abbreviated version of what I told Flor. Outlining my newfound abilities, as Florence put it, and mentioning how she is maintaining my existence. I briefly contemplated leaving that part out, because it feels private somehow, a special bond that we share. However, William would start to get suspicious when I wasn't returning as often as I need to the Shadows.

Nodding, William says, "I suspected as much, and I can see I wasn't far off base. I am weary of you harvesting energy from my daughter, yet it doesn't seem to have any ill effect. You will have to forgive me for being protective, and, of course, I will continue to monitor your behavior. You haven't been back that long, and you are the first of your kind. We need to understand exactly what we are dealing with."

"I understand," I say, knowing I will chafe under their close supervision but cannot blame their caution.

Gregg pipes up from over by the map, "I think we've got a good plan to get everyone to the surface if we're done with all the hushed meetings."

"Comin'" Samson grunts as he gets to his feet, and William pats my shoulder before we join the others.

"Aggie is going to walk you through the operation," Thierry says.

Taking the lead, Aggie outlines the plan. "Alright, everybody, listen up. We have four main pockets of survivors. They are circled on the map." She takes a moment to point out each. "Since we remain undetected in the tunnels, we are going to bring them here before we go topside. Aric thinks we should take them up through the courtyard and into the Keep that way. We can assess the damage and then decide if we should lift the door to the basement. They know we are returning and will be ready to move.

"We will split into four teams and move simultaneously. Aric and Thierry, you'll fetch the furthest group. They are the hardest to get to and since Aric has already been there, it will take less time. There is one injured man that you'll have to carry, Thierry. Gregg you'll go with Wallace back to where we found him, he knows the way. Samson and William, I'm sending you to get the easiest group. It is a straight shot down the tunnel we are in, so you shouldn't have an issue. Lucian, you and I will go after the remaining individuals. They are located closest to the Keep but more importantly, closest to the gate. Based on the snippets of conversation I've heard, you can tell when something comes out of Shadows and you'll be our early warning system. Any questions?"

"Yeah," Florence raises her hand. "What am I supposed to do?" She asks, sounding upset. I can't tell if it is from being left out of the plan or something else entirely.

"You'll be here to receive our new guests. They will need food and water, that is where you come in," Aggie speaks like she is talking to a child. Florence just clenches her fists and nods. "Any other questions? I'd like to be on the move in ten minutes."

Everyone looks around shaking their heads. "Good. Pair off, go over your routes and arm yourselves. We can't be too careful."

Breaking off into our teams we prepare to leave. Florence is speaking in a hushed voice to her father when Aggie saunters over. "Ok, pretty boy, we do things my way and we move quickly, save the flirting for when we get back," she winks at me.

"Flirting?" I raise a brow while checking my blades.

"Come on now, we both know she can't handle you," she says, indicating Florence. "And seeing as we are the best-looking people in this room, it is only natural we'd end up a little flirtatious."

"And here I thought we were paired off because you needed my skills."

"Oh no, those are still needed, I just also couldn't pass up the opportunity for a little alone time," she says, running a hand down my arm.

"I'm flattered Aggie." I say, removing her hand, "but I think the priority should be getting everyone back safely."

"Fair enough, but you'll come around," is all she says before she walks over to where she laid her weapons.

I look around for Flor, to make sure she will be all right here by herself when I see her come out of the root cellar with an arm full of supplies. Setting them down, she brushes hair away from her face and pulls the dagger out from her pocket sitting it next to a bag of dried fruit.

"We need to find you a belt for that," I say, pointing to the weapon.

"Yeah, Thierry said I should check the closets in the hall while everyone's gone."

"Your job is just as important as ours, Florence," I tell her, sensing her sadness, I know she wants to feel useful.

"Sure, it is," she says rolling her eyes. "Have fun with miss know-it-all over there."

I watch her snap open a blanket, irritated. If I didn't know any better, I'd say she was jealous instead of angry for being left behind. That thought brings a smile to my face, and I'm about to tease her for it when Aggie appears behind us.

"Time to go, handsome." I know she only says it to get a rise out of Florence, but it works. Flor balls up the blanket she just opened and glares daggers at Aggie's back.

"We will be back before you know it," I say, trying to ease the tension. "Shut the door behind us and find a belt for that dagger so it is easier to access should something happen."

"I will," she says, absently reaching for it. "Come back safe, ok? I still have to show you up in a sparing contest." She looks like she might hug me, but instead punches my shoulder like we are old buddies.

I grab her hand and let the dark magic within me tug on the energy flowing through her. The resulting sensation is intoxicating. Her pupils dilate, and I can feel her pulse quicken. "Nothing is going to happen to me," I reassure her, leaning a little closer.

She meets me halfway, a moth flying too close to the flame. Her eyes become hooded and I glance at her lips, her tongue darting out to moisten them. Our breaths mingle.

She smells of lavender and rain. I am ensnared and close the remaining distance.

Our lips touch and my blood has been lit on fire. Scorching trails of crackling energy zip between our lips, racing down my arms and legs, churning in my gut.

Someone claps their hands, and the moment is broken. Florence sucks in a breath and leans away, busying herself with the blanket she dropped, shielding her face from view.

We are both panting, and she looks at me with a desperate plea, glow fading from her eyes.

Thierry claps his hands again and gives me a censuring look. "We all know where we are headed?"

"Yes," we say in unison. I'm not sure where I'm going, but Aggie will be in the lead. I plan on shutting down her misguided attempts on the way if she didn't just witness that life-altering kiss.

"Then let's get this over with. It should be morning by the time we get everyone back and up to the courtyard. No dawdling and report anything suspicious. Let's move." Thierry opens the door to the sewers, and we all file out.

I take one last look at Florence who is fingering her lips. My own tingle in response, as if she were touching them as well. She catches my eye and gives me a small wave before I follow behind Aggie. Shock written all over her face.

I hear the door click shut and for reasons I cannot understand, miss the steady hum that comes with her nearness. Now that we are not in a shared space, the absence of her energy is rattling. I did not realize I could feel the underlying current of her until I am forced to be without it.

Chapter 17
Florence

The silence is unforgiving after everyone scatters into the underground tunnels. My blood is roaring in my ears, and my lips twitch. I feel like I've been electrocuted and lightening now lives in my veins. The connection we just shared was more than a simple kiss. It was loaded with questions, but also answers.

An electrifying moment that felt like a promise, an apology and a declaration wrapped into one.

The simple act shook my foundation. Lucian's reaction mirrored my own when we broke apart. Stars shone out of his luminous eyes and his breathing was erratic. As the glow dissipated, I caught a glimpse of the vulnerable boy broken by the Shadows.

Heaving out a sigh, I rub at the constant ache that has returned to my chest. My nerves are shot, and I miss Lucian's calming presence. I refold the blanket I've crumpled and look for something else to keep me occupied, ignoring the urge to replay that kiss over and over in my mind.

I decide to look for a belt for my father's dagger. I should probably give it back to him, but he hasn't asked to see it after using it to punctuate the note he left.

Opening the first closet, I am assaulted by the smell of stale cloth. Linens and old uniforms are molding against the limestone in the back. Everything in the front seems to be a little moth eaten but otherwise clean. Shutting the cloth back in, I move on to the next. This one smells of leather and metal. I should find what I am looking for here and start methodically pulling everything out. There is every weapon imaginable: short swords, daggers, broad swords, knives, throwing stars, chains, maces and axes; it is a warrior's dream.

A row of belts along the right side catches my eye, and I look to see if there is one that will fit my waist. The last one I pull is thinner than the others. Light brown leather that is beautifully engraved with replicating knots, like the outside of my father's cloak. It appears to have been made for a woman, and I try it on. The fit is almost perfect, I'm thicker than the original wearer but I can secure it through the first hole. Pulling the Seraphim Blade from my pocket it slides right into the loop on the side. Perfect.

I have no need to look in the other two closets but, curiosity gets the best of me. Parchment and medical supplies fill up the next. It smells a little like mildew, yet nothing looks in disrepair. I make a note of where things are in this one in case any of the survivors need bandages or healing salves. Shutting the door, I shamble to the final door.

I am not prepared for what this one holds. I am overwhelmed by the scent of copper and immediately regret my curious nature. This isn't just a closet but a whole room, filled to the brim with instruments of torture. A giant cage surrounded by ominous looking stains takes up a good portion of the middle. A crude rack sits along the back wall, flanked by chains with cuffs attached. Pokers, clamps, saws and screws are lined up like soldiers in neat rows atop a table off to the side.

Everything looks clean, like it has been organized recently. Under the oppressive odor of dried blood, I detect a sterile, almost clean smell. This room has definitely been in use, but why? What would a torture chamber be used for when the enemies of the Seraphim Order are incorporeal, dark magic wielding monsters? Do Samson and my father know about this? What about Lucian? He knew how to get into the basement, maybe he knows why this is here?

I shudder as I shut out the horrible images this place conjures. I feel like this should have been locked and realize it is designed to look like any other closet to discourage any prying eyes. The inside of the door doesn't have a handle and matches the walls. This was well thought out.

I refuse to believe my father would condone the torture of any living being, enemy or not. I feel sick to my stomach as I walk back out to the main room. The urge to flee and see this sky is almost overwhelming. It's too much.

The familiar click of the secret latch pulls my attention. Samson shoulders open the door and a group of about fifteen men, women and a couple children walk in with my father at the rear. They look scared and utterly defeated. Ash coats their clothing. No one appears to be injured, which is a good thing, but none will look me directly in the eye.

"Grab them some water, Flossy," says my father while he shuts the door. Hurrying to pass out the flasks, I catch Samson eyeing the belt around my waist.

"It seems ye and yer mother had a similar taste. She had a belt jus' like that," Samson remarks. My father takes me in for the first time.

"You look just like her, pet."

"I think I look more like you, aither." I fiddle with the belt, adjusting and readjusting it.

"You've her eyes and fair skin. With the hunter's belt and dagger, you're a spitting image, all stubborn beauty." His eyes soften as a smile plays across his lips. Remembering the others in the room, I check and make sure the water has made the rounds and everyone has a place to sit. Samson is busy passing out rations of dried beef, fruit and nuts.

Now all we can do is wait for everyone else. I want to ask about the room I discovered but dare not with so many people around. These villagers have already witnessed enough bloodshed. I don't need to add another instance of brutality to the list.

A blush heats my cheeks under his assessment. "Did you see any of the others?"

"No, we didn't. We moved as quickly as possible, everyone else should be along shortly. We didn't have far to go, just right down the tunnel as Aggie said."

It feels like hours pass before the door clicks again. This time Gregg and Wallace enter with twenty more survivors. The water and rations are passed around again, and it is difficult to move about the space. I don't know how we are going to fit more people into this basement.

"Once those of ye have had a breather, I'll be takin whoever is able up ta tha courtyard of the Keep. There hasn't been much activity on tha surface, fars we can tell, and it should be daylight. Get ye some fresh air, make room for tha rest," Samson announces once the second group has settled in, he shrewdly leaves out the part where Lucian and I were ambushed.

"Are you sure it is safe?" A woman in the back shouts. Clearly the idea of coming out of hiding isn't too appealing.

"There are others?" Someone else asks.

"We canna stay in these tunnels if we want ta get ye outta ta city. And yes, there are others." Murmurs sound throughout the crowd at the possibility of friends or family being found.

"But where will we go? We have nothing left?" A man with a long beard counters.

My father interjects, abating the man's worries. "There will be time to salvage what we can and find you supplies to carry you to Glanchester to the North. We will need someone to ride ahead, tell them what has happened here and prepare them for refugees. Thierry has already written a missive to the Seraphim Order in that city," he says, touching his chest where the letter must be stowed. "Those of you who wish to stay below can. For now, everyone else follow Samson to the courtyard."

Much to my surprise, most follow Samson out to the Keep. Three remain, a woman and two children, who appear to be her own. Picking up two flasks I kneel before the youngest. Hiding within her mother's skirts she looks terrified and unsure. "Hello there, my name is Florence. Would you like some water?" I ask gently. Turning her face away I can't tell if she is shy or frightened of me. "I promise I am not here to hurt you, dear. I am here to help. What is your name?"

Giving me half of her face, she blinks wide brown eyes at me. "I'm Iseabal," she answers tentatively.

"Ah, what a pretty name for a pretty girl." A bashful smile greets me before she snatches the water from my hand.

Looking at the older boy, Iseabal's mother introduces him, "This is my son, Tomas, and I am Una. I thank you for your kindness and for finding us. My husband ushered us underground before joining other townsfolk to fight the flames. He did not return and I -" her lip trembles, and I can see the grief in her eyes. "We do not think he made it," she whispers.

"I am so sorry Una," for that is all I can say. I understand loss, but to have lost so much so quickly is unfathomable. My heart goes out this woman and her children. They have suffered needlessly in a war that is not their own. My resolve to fight hardens within me. I will do everything in my power to free this world of the Reapers and their creatures.

I will learn who I am and what I can do to make sure this never happens again.

"We will make this right," I promise. "I will not stop until the Reapers are banished from this land."

I briefly touch Iseabal's cheek and move to stand with my father, who also remained to wait for the others. "You will teach me all I need to know about who I am, aither. I will not see these deaths and this town's misery go unanswered. If I am the key, so be it."

Pride shines out of his eyes as he responds to my sudden declaration. "Your mother would be so proud of you, Flossy. I am proud of you. Where most would falter in the face of adversity, you have handled it with grace and determination. I can see the fire in your eyes and believe me, we will fight. But we must prepare. Getting everyone safely to Glanchester is our first priority. You will learn along the way, and we will be ready."

"Aye, papa," I use the term of endearment I haven't used since I turned into a young woman, and it brings an even bigger smile to his face, tears shimmering in his eyes.

Right then, Thierry and Aric stumble through the door with a burly man between them. Followed by more forlorn townsfolk. Una's children seem to be the only young that have survived out of those who have returned. My heart breaks even further for Darkwell. Setting the man down, Thierry rushes to the medical closet and pulls out several bandages. The man they carried in is sprawled out on the floor, bleeding from a wound on his leg. It appears to have been crushed, and I swallow back bile.

"What's happened? Step aside, I am a healer." Una forces Aric out of the way and Iseabal startles me by grabbing my hand. Tomas is right behind her watching his mother.

"Beams from the smithy pinned his leg," Thierry blurts trying to wrap a bandage around the man's leg. Sweat beads on the injured smith's brow, and his jaw is locked in pain, at least he is conscious.

"Och, stop that, the wound needs cleaned." Smacking Thierry's hand, Una grabs a discarded flask and barks instructions. "Find me more water, bandages, yarrow, if you have it, and for this man's sake, some hemlock and poppy." I step off to the side with Tomas and Iseabal in tow to let their mother work. I am amazed at her skill and commanding air. I will have to see if she can teach me more about the art of healing.

I settle the children on a nearby blanket and try not to let my mind wander to Lucian. He hasn't returned yet, and I've been worried.

As if sensing my distress, my father wraps me in a small embrace. "He will be back soon, Flossy. They just needed to be extra careful where they were going."

"I know papa, I'm sure they will be back shortly," I say, hugging him back.

Samson returns to take more of the survivors to the surface and Una has the smith's leg bandaged. He is knocked out with a concoction of hemlock and poppy, lethal in large enough doses, but in the correct amount, can ease the pain of one who suffers.

"He should be out for a while. Getting him to the courtyard might be a challenge, but for now he should be fine." Una wipes her hands on her apron, returning to her children.

Thierry thanks her and confers with my father about who will ride ahead to Glanchester.

My mood sours the longer I wait for Lucian. I am trying to be patient, but the longer they are gone, the more on edge I feel. My mind returns to the torture chamber and images of broken bodies rattling the chains fill my head.

Chapter 18
Lucian

Aggie sets a fast clip through the tunnels, deftly dodging debris and stagnant water. We've been snaking our way through the sewers, and I must admit I've gotten turned around.

"How much further?" I ask, trailing behind her. The sun has started to rise, and the light reaches us through the evenly spaced drains above.

"We are almost there, patience," she calls back to me. The vermin appear to have fled the sewers, we haven't crossed a single rat or mouse. The fires must've driven them out of the city, or they are bunked with the survivors knowing they might find food. I can't imagine where this group must be, but Aggie said they are closest to the Keep, probably on the other side near the port.

I expected her to be more cautious this close to the gate, but she is making enough noise to rouse a sleeping bear. Odd that. Usually Fae move with a natural grace that allows them to pass nearly undetected to the untrained ear. Perhaps she wishes for the survivors to hear our approach, so they won't be frightened. That is what I would do, heavens know they have been through enough of an ordeal, and we do not need to startle them.

"There is chamber up ahead, that is where we are headed," Aggie points as she breaks into a jog. I listen through our pounding footsteps and hear nothing. No muffled conversations or the rustle of clothing beside our own. I cannot detect another soul in this part of the tunnels. Maybe the survivors are too scared to talk, or they are no longer alive.

That thought kicks my heart into overdrive. What if we are too late and the Reapers discovered their hideout? I am not sure I could forgive myself, or the others for not bringing them to us sooner.

Turning a corner, I see a small, wooden door up ahead. The dampness of the tunnels has eaten through the bottom and the bars across a small window look like they are rusting. What a bizarre place for an isolated room. There is no light filtering out and I am about to voice my concerns when Aggie stops and places a finger over her lips to silence my questions.

Approaching the door, she raises her hand as if to knock. With speed I wasn't expecting she rounds on me and cracks me across the face. Reeling backward, I catch myself before I fall, but she is already on top of me driving her fists into my head and chest. Becoming part of the Shadows has its advantages, and I return her swift blows, matching her tenacity.

"You must be more Shadow than I realized, handsome. You should've been knocked out by that first hit," she says through clenched teeth. I have managed to shove her off of me, and we are standing facing one another. "I guess I will just have to try harder."

Becoming a wraith, she strikes behind my right leg. It buckles and my knee slams into the ground. Grunting, I try to stand back up, but she kicks out my left, and I sprawl onto the ground.

To say I am confused, is an understatement. I don't have time to ask what in the name of the Three Kingdoms she is doing, because the next thing I know, she is kneeling on my chest, staring down at me with triumph in her eyes.

"Nighty night pretty boy," her right hand descends, and right before contact I see a rock in her hand. Pain explodes from my temple and black dots dance across my eyes. Rearing back, she lands another strike, and the world goes black.

There is something sticky coating my eyes, and I can feel my pulse throbbing through my head. A metronome of drips ring in my ears, and my limbs feel as though they weigh one-thousand stone. Getting my eyes open needs to be step one. Figuring out what the hell happened and where I am, will be steps two and three.

Blinking against the slime across my eyelids is a challenge. I go to wipe it away when the rattle of chains joins the steady drip. This must be the reason for the heavy feeling. I am able to get one eye open and realize the other is swollen shut. My legs are tingling, and I can tell I am sitting propped up against limestone walls.

A sharp pain in my wrists elicits a hiss through my teeth, and I look down to see I am shackled to the wall I am leaning against. The chains wrap around the outside of my shirt sleeves, but a small patch of skin has been singed and has begun to smoke, the odor stinging my nostrils. Atrum. The metal used to destroy Reapers. This was planned. It may not kill me, but it will weaken my abilities.

Suddenly, everything comes crashing back.

Our roundabout trek through the tunnels, the wooden door and finally Aggie knocking me out.

We have been betrayed.

I don't know how deep this deception runs, but I know for certain at least the twins are working against us. I cannot understand why, and I need to get out of here to warn the others.

I think of Florence and start to struggle. Pulling on the chains does little and only makes my wrists burn worse. I need to calm down and formulate a plan, injuring myself further will not help anyone. I pull the sleeves of my shirt down as best I can without doing any more damage and start to think.

Taking in my surroundings I see a large cage in front of me. A table with metal objects takes up the majority of one of the walls and there is a stretching rack next to me. The only thing I'm sure of at the moment is that I am in a torture chamber. Even more secrets to unravel. The bitch must've dragged me in here after she attacked me, Fae strength aiding her.

I need to find a way out of these chains and out of this room. The door to the tunnels must've been a facade because I don't see anything resembling a door in this room. Another trick and another trap.

I could yell for help, but what good would that do? I don't know where I am and the chances of anyone hearing me are almost laughable. They would've made sure I was far enough away that I couldn't be easily tracked. Separation is key.

The first thing I need to focus on is getting these shackles off, but so far it seems hopeless. There is nothing on the ground I can use as a pick and I've been relieved of my weapons.

TL Hoffman

The cold reality sets in.

I am trapped underground in an undisclosed location, bound by the one thing I cannot combat. The nefarious plans of the twins may run deep within in the Seraphim Order, and the focal point is Florence and her abilities to create portals into the Shadows. I will die here if I cannot find a way to free myself. Florence has been keeping me alive and without her or a gateway, I will not be able to regenerate. The tingling has already begun in my legs.

I am running out of time.

Chapter 19
Florence

The rest of the survivors have been moved to the courtyard. Getting the injured smithy up the ladder took some creative maneuvering, but the men managed to do it. Una and her children are settling into the kitchen of the Keep while the rest are foraging for what they can.

They have decided to send Gregg and Wallace ahead to deliver the news of the city's fall and prepare Glanchester for the remains of Darkwell. Gregg needs better medical attention than we can give, the wound in his head refusing to heal, and Wallace was hard pressed to let him leave alone. An unspoken attachment between the two is palpable. Gregg was explaining to me how fortunate they were to find Wallace within the tunnels, he was too worried about him to mind the beam that knocked him unconscious.

I find the bond between the two a wondrous thing.

I keep my eye on the trap door, awaiting Lucian's return. I'm not able to put my finger on how I know, but I sense something is wrong. I can feel it. I unknowingly became so accustom to our connection that being without it is like being starved of oxygen.

I could feel him through the tunnels for a moment but lost him the further away they went. All of a sudden, his constant pulse was ripped from my conscience, an essential part snuffed out.

Jealously of Aggie may be coloring my thoughts, but I do not trust her. She and her twin have a similar aloofness that causes me to be weary. I find it hard to believe they couldn't defend Kalligan against the Reaper onslaught inside the Keep. Separate, they are a force, but together they must be unstoppable. The more I think about it, the more suspicious I become. Perhaps I should talk to Samson, see what he thinks of the two Fae among us.

A head of beautiful blond hair emerges from the depths of the tunnels. Flopping on the ground, Aggie rolls over. I can see her clothes are torn and one of her eyes is discolored.

Oh no.

I fall on my knees beside her, "Papa! Samson! Come quickly, Aggie has been attacked!" I grab her shoulders and begin checking over her.

My father and Samson tear out of the kitchen with Una not far behind. The Fae is looking around wildly as her mouth open and closes. "Aggie! Look at me! Where is Lucian?" I am shaking her now. I continue to look towards the hole to the tunnels but no one else climbs above.

The other three have slid in beside us and assess Aggie. Aric is in the kitchen doorway, unconcerned and moving slowing in our direction. He looks almost pleased.

"I - I don't know what happened. One minute I was leading, running through the tunnels, then all of a sudden, I was struck from behind. I was able to get myself turned around, and Lucian was pinning me down, striking my face. I threw him off of me, but he got in a few good hits before he fled. Took off running toward the bay. I think he is planning on taking a boat across the sea, kept asking if the harbor had burned..." she looks at me then at the surrounding group.

"Didn't you say he knew his way through the sewers, Samson?"

"Aye, tha lad's tha one that led us ta the basement."

"There was something a little off about him." Thierry says, rubbing the back of his neck.

I cannot believe what I am hearing. Lucian betrayed us? Was he just using me to get as far as Darkwell then flee? Was that why he saw me that day, brought me back from the Shadows, he was working with the Reapers? Doubts creep in, clawing their way through my denials. I may not trust Aggie, but I cannot discount her appearance. Lucian would be one of the few that could overpower her, take her unaware.

Sitting on my haunches I can feel my father staring at me. I don't want him to see my disappointment, so I focus on Una.

"How's your eyesight? Watch my finger." She moves her index finger in front of Aggie's eyes, monitoring how they track the movement. "Your head seems to be fine, other than some bruising. Did he get you anywhere else?"

"Just a few knocks on my chest but nothing that won't heal quickly," rolling her shoulders she goes to stand.

Samson and Thierry help her up and she turns to me. "I'm sorry Florence, I tried to stop him, but he was determined." All I can do is nod as my heart sinks.

"We canna be worryin' about where tha lads gone now. We need ta get these people on tha road before tha day gets any later," Samson declares, walking off to check the supplies.

Aric finally checks on his sister and everyone gives me apologetic looks before going back to their tasks.

"Papa, this doesn't feel right." I say when we are alone.

"He fooled us all Flossy, including me. We can't dwell on it now though. We need to get somewhere safe and begin preparing for the next attack. Come on," he closes the door to the tunnels and leads me toward the kitchen. "There are still some provisions that haven't been ruined we need to pack. Wallace and Gregg are set to leave shortly."

I am still having difficulty believing that Lucian would just leave us. Thoughts swirl around me, as I try to make sense of it. Our connection had been so real, so palpable. I pace through the memories, searching for hints of betrayal and come up empty. Even from the beginning he was trying to protect me. He is either the best actor I've ever met, or there is something I am not seeing. Something I am missing.

Keeping my panic from surfacing is difficult, as I replay every conversation, every quiet moment.

I feel as though I've been abandoned all over again. Lost at sea after a violent storm, nothing but the stars to guide me. The shock is jarring and dismantles me.

A shout goes up from the far end of the courtyard, Thierry is watching over the wall, searching for signs of life. "Oy, I see a few horses by the center of town."

"Those must be our mounts," I say, racing over to where Thierry is climbing down from a ladder. "Is one a Namidian? There should be two smaller horses as well."

"Aye, they are grazing through the refuse. Are those the horses you rode in on?"

"Yes. The Namidian was Lucian's, I believe he called him Javai," I am surprised he would leave that beautiful horse.

"I'm going to get them for Wallace and Gregg. They can utilize the smaller two, Namidian's can be temperamental so we must me cautious." He leaves through a small door in the side of the courtyard.

I climb up the ladder to watch him track the horses. Javai notices his approach first, ears flicking in agitation. Thierry manages to grab the reins of the two smaller mounts and brings them back to the doorway. Tying them to a flipped-over cart, he returns for Lucian's horse. Javai is weary of the stranger's approach and backs up toward an alleyway. Thierry moves slowly, but the Namidian bolts, escaping towards the docks.

At least we were able to get the other two for Gregg and Wallace, they seem to not mind who rides them. I meet Thierry outside and stroke the pretty mare I rode. Men's voices carry across the open doorway, and the two messengers appear, packs and weapons ready. The bandage around Gregg's head looks fresh, and they have a day's worth of rations stuffed in a saddlebag.

"Couldn't catch the Namidian, but these two should service," Thierry says, patting the grey's flank.

"We will ride as quick as we can. Got the letter here," Gregg thumps his pocket. "Everyone else should be ready to leave within the hour." Wallace straps the saddlebag to the black horse and swings himself up.

"Be careful, ride straight through, and raise hell if they won't grant you a meeting. They don't know what is coming for them," Thierry claps Gregg on the back before the other man mounts the grey and they are off. I watch as they ride toward the city gates and push my anxiety to the side, I refuse to think about Lucian.

We shut ourselves back in the courtyard where everyone is preparing to leave. They have the smithy set up in the remnants of an old cart that a few of the larger men will pull. It will be slow going, but at least they will be out of the city. Weapons have been pulled from the store rooms downstairs, along with food and flasks of water. The party is big enough that any roadside outlaw won't bother them, and they have little in the way of possessions, offering nothing but terrified looks and dried meat.

Samson comes over to run through the plan. "Thierry will lead 'em out since he is now tha highest rankin' Order member. Una and her children will travel close to tha injured smithy. That way she can keep an eye on him and those two can hitch a ride when they tire. You, yer father, Aric, Aggie and meself will bring up tha rear once they've made good headway. Thierry wants us to do a final sweep o' tha city before we abandon her completely. Aric and Aggie will make quick work of tha majority, and we can cover the rest. We've got provisions packed, and this lot should be headin' out once Thierry is ready."

"Are we going to search for Lucian?" I hesitantly ask. I know they want to make sure we haven't left anyone behind and I can't help but feel like we will be looking for something specific.

Samson squints at me and clips his response, "nay lass. He's as good as gone, ye best forget tha' boy."

"I'm just finding it hard to believe he would leave us like this," I argue, searching his gaze.

"Believe it, Florence," he huffs before stalking away. I've never known Samson to be this way before, short and abrupt, automatically dismissing my fears. Must be the stress of this journey. All we have to go on is adrenaline and the information before us.

That must be it.

Distracting myself, I assist Una in settling the smithy onto the cart and cover the man with a blanket. He is awake but drowsy from the poppy and hemlock. Tomas lifts Iseabel onto the cart and turns to me. "We will see you in Glanchester, won't we?"

"Of course, you will, Tomas. Take care of your mom and Iseabel. They will need you on this tough journey," I squeeze his shoulder and hug Una. "Be well."

Thierry motions for everyone to pay attention and looks over the motley bunch. Most are capable men and women who had the chance to escape underground. They did not hesitate to find safety because they had no one but themselves to protect. Still covered in ash and dirt, they look to Thierry for guidance. "Alright troupe. We have a decent journey ahead to Glanchester. We will need to camp but must move quickly to make it a good distance from the city. I will lead and those with any combat experience have already been told where they will be among our ranks. Keep alert and stay with me. We cannot afford to have any stragglers, and if you fall behind the cart, we will move without you. Understood?"

A chorus of ayes goes up around the courtyard. There are roughly thirty souls about the leave Darkwell for good, less than the original estimate. The rest have been lost to the devastation or have not been found. My heart aches that so few remain.

"Aric, Aggie, Samson, William and Florence will meet us at the first checkpoint where we will camp for the night. If they are not there, we will move without them and hope they catch up," Thierry makes eye contact with each of us before he addresses the group one more time. "I cannot stress enough how quickly we must move, Glanchester needs to be warned and will need all the help they can get. Be prepared to be pushed. Let's move." Adjusting the pack he carries, he turns to lead the survivors single file out of the courtyard.

I cast a quick prayer to anyone listening to keep them safe and hope the Reapers do not return. Once the last person is out, Samson waits in the doorway, watching them make their way to the city gates. It is a long time before Samson turns and shuts the door.

"They've made it ta tha gate." My shoulders relax, and I await further instructions. Samson glances in the direction of the twins and strides up to my father. "I am sorry Will, for everythin'. Boy, was I surprised ta see ya show up, back from tha dead. I'd love ta bring ye on board, but ye weren't part of the plan."

Moving with preternatural speed, Aric grabs my father from behind. Gripping his forehead to expose his neck, the Fae rips a dagger from my father's belt and drags the blade across his throat. Blood gushes from the wound, a wet gurgle the only sound as his body slumps to the ground.

Chapter 20
Florence

I cannot move. I cannot breathe.

I look on in horror as his life seeps from his neck onto the ground, leaching out around his body. Like a morbid puppet, my father stares lifelessly at the clouds, eyes gone glassy, mouth open like he may yet speak.

Finally, instinct takes over, and I start to scream. "Papa!!" I'm wailing incoherently as I crawl to him. Tears haze my vision, and I'm picked up from behind, a hand effectively cutting off my cries.

"We can't have you waking the neighbors, dove," Aric whispers into my ear. His breath is hot on the side of my face and it feels as though he is breathing fire. I realize he is wiping the blade on my skirt, my father's blood smeared across the filth covering my dress. Will the agony never end? I just got him back, and now he is gone again. Really gone.

Aggie tsks, "We are always doing your dirty work, Samson. You're lucky the queen sent us to keep an eye on you or things would never get done. First, we had to deal with Kalligan and now William." She toes my father's body with her boot, and I struggle against Aric.

"William was supposed ta be dead already, Agatha. It isn't my fault he returned."

"Technically, it is. And don't call me Agatha, I hate that. But you should've double checked the day he washed down river. That is beside the point. He is very much dead now, no thanks to you or the Reapers you allied us with." She looks over at me and a wicked grin spreading across her face, "What are we to do with sweet, gifted Florence here?"

"Her use isn't done. Ye know that, so stop toying with her. She will be opening up more doors to tha Shadows fer us." He is bent over William's body, checking his pockets. "She is the key."

"Well yes, but I think we should have a little fun with her," at that, I start to struggle harder. Lucian has betrayed me and now Samson? I'm not sure how much more I can withstand.

There is a buzzing that has begun beneath my skin, pushing, seeking a way out. My hands are on fire, and I'm still trying to escape Aric's iron hold.

"Ah there we are, there is the fight. Would you look at that, her eyes are glowing," Aggie is studying me like an experiment, and Aric's arms are only getting tighter. I can't get a breath, and his giant paw is still covering my mouth.

"She is reaching into the void, drawing on the energy from the Shadows. If she takes enough o' it, a gateway will open. That is how she looked when we'd wake her from tha dreams. Hold tight, we're about ta have visitors." The man I've known my whole life has been replaced by someone else. I barely recognize the cold glint in Samson's eyes as he watches the courtyard, waiting for something.

My skin has begun to prickle everywhere like a limb when it becomes numb. The intensity is making my blood boil. My vision is wavering, and I am not sure I can contain whatever is building within me.

Squeezing my eyes shut, I push at the roar in my veins and like a crack of thunder before a downpour, the pressure releases. Aric is flung away from me, and Aggie and Samson go flying. Wind rushes around my body and whips my skirts and hair into a frenzy.

Opening my eyes, I see that I am surrounded by a pale green glow that sparks and zaps at nearby objects. The tingling has subsided and the air stills. As my clothing settles, the glow slowly trickles into my chest, returning to me.

I have never felt so alive. I should be terrified of what I've just done but I am not.

A black orb lazily circles my fingers, tucking itself into my sleeve.

"I guess we just had ta overload her system and her powers surface. Papa's death did tha trick." Samson says, struggling to his feet.

"It's like a defense mechanism. She goes off like a bomb," Aggie adds.

"Ripped a nice hole in the veil while she was at it," Aric gestures behind me.

Stiffly, I turn around and can barely make out a shimmering outline. Beyond, the colors are muted, and a blast of cold air strikes me in the face. What have I done?

"That should suffice ta bring Gabriel through," Samson says, muffled voice sounding small through the roar in my ears.

A high-pitched scream rents the air. The ground trembles and slow, rhythmic beats sound in the distance, growing ever louder. Through the broken air a shadow circles, and another cry travels through, much closer this time.

Heart pounding, I round on Samson, pulling my dagger from its place at my hip, "What is happening Samson, what have you done?" There are so many things I wish to say but cannot get them through the lump in my throat. I am numb, and I may never trust another person again. I'll be lucky if I make it out of this day alive and do not care, I need answers and I need them now.

"It should be what have ye done... I am ushering in a new era, Florence. One where I will rule all of tha Three Kingdoms under one banner and the Reapers will reign. My patience is about ta be rewarded."

"What are you talking about, Samson? This isn't who you are."

"Isn't it?" As I watch, the light in his eyes becomes unhinged. He has drawn his own weapon now and is heading toward the entrance to the Shadows. "I've been waiting years fer this day, ever since I knew yer parents would keep their precious little Halfling," he spits, sounding disgusted. "I was never as good as them, always workin' in their shadow. Ever since we were young, yer father was better than me at everythin'. He was tha better fighter, tha better tracker, had better luck with women. The minute we both laid eyes on yer mother we both wanted her. But she chose yer father. It was infuriating. But then ye were conceived, and I knew ye would be the answer ta me problems. I spent some time away from yer parents after they retired to Grimsfield, traveling, searching. Eventually, I found meself in the presence of tha Unseelie Queen in Isiwen and she had tha answers I was seeking."

My mind latches onto the title, Unseelie Queen. The fabled leader of the Dark Fae. In the legends, the Fae are split into two courts, Seelie and Unseelie. Light and Dark. From what I've read, the Light Fae of the Seelie court are beautiful and shun all things imperfect. The Dark Fae fo the Unseelie court love to cause trouble and their appearance is malformed, at times grotesque. The queen must be a true sight to behold, oozing power and maleficence. If she helped Samson with his diabolical plan, she must wish for chaos, hoping his plans come to fruition, where dark magic rules the land.

Samson is still pontificating when I refocus on his words. "I needed power and power she gave. Ye see, I now control the Reapers. You could say they are loyal ta me and only me. I needed an army, and she provided one. As long as I remain faithful ta her, I get everythin' I want, and her court can finally come out from beneath the mountain. She may have skimmed some years off me life for insurance, but it will be worth it, fer I'll be immortal in the end. And you, my dear Florence, will help me open endless gateways.

"I have been granted power, and it was no mistake those three came for ye all those years ago, I willed it so. They were supposed ta lure you out through those dreams and take ye into the Shadows. But of course, yer parents had to intervene, took me five years ta break through that damn barrier. Once I did, it was no coincidence that Reaper found ye back in Grimsfield. Yer cursed Father showing up, leavin' notes, was no' part of the plan, although his death seems to have awoken yer potential.

"So, I had ta change course, get ye away from him before he discovered me true intent. But his arrival made this plan so much better. I was able ta get word to tha twins, and they took care of Kalligan fer me. Opening tha portal ta destroy Darkwell, expediting tha process. I planned ta get ye on me side, be my Conduit by choice, see things the way I see them. Dear old papa and Lucian derailed that, so you'll be workin' under duress," he smiles maniacally at me.

"I will not do it! I can't believe this. I trusted you! And you created all this death, over a woman" I say, incredulous. "My parents loved you..." I add in a small voice, deflating.

"Never wound a man's pride, Flossy."

"You don't get to call me that."

"You'll come 'round once you meet Gabriel. And if ye don't, we'll go back ta the forcing part."

"I would rather die," I say, raising my dagger in challenge, fight renewing.

"You don't want ta ride tha high of opening a portal, Florence? I saw tha look on yer face. Pure ecstasy. Power has tha ability to corrupt even the best of men. Ye will be no different."

The constant beat, like that of a drum, is upon us, deafening in its intensity. My ears pop as the portal opens further, a slashing maw ripping through the air.

"Join us Florence. Rule on high with tha Keeper of Souls," Samson has his arms spread out and is basking in the disorder I've created.

"You want to rule a Kingdom of the dead?" I yell over the constant beat.

"Better that than a Kingdom of the damned and tha spoiled. This world needs a change and I plan ta introduce these petty civilians to it. They will bow before me or be ripped from this existence."

The cold is descending and the Shadows seep into the courtyard. I have to figure out how to stop it.

Samson and the twins are distracted by the ever-growing opening which gives me an opportunity to look about for another weapon. Something catches my eye on my father's body, peeking out from the waist in his trousers. Samson must have missed it in his crazed state.

Keeping my eyes on the portal, I make my way back to him and lift his shirt higher. Tucked into his belt is a dagger matching my own. This must be the Seraphim Blade

Samson was looking for when we ran. It must be my mother's. My father has kept it this whole time.

I turn it over and hold it loosely in my left hand, mimicking the way Lucian handled his two scimitars earlier. Thinking about him gives me pause. What if he didn't abandon us and, Aggie actually killed him?

I wasn't sure I could feel more pain, but there it is, right where my heart should be. I quickly bury the hurt and am left raw and broken. An eerie calm descends, and I feel nothing. My heart has become a shrunken mass pumping blood through my veins and nothing more.

I might reopen the box I have shoved my grief in someday, but not today.

Today is not like every other day. I will take control of my future, my life.

I am more, and I do have a calling.

Squaring my shoulders, I chant a new mantra, "Samson, will pay. For my father. For my mother. For Lucian."

I can do this. I need to figure out how I can undo what I've done and do it without getting killed. I have to warn Glanchester.

Movement from the tower pulls my attention and several Reapers are climbing down from the battlements. That must be where the other gateway is located. Focusing back on the rift I created, a shadow darts through with an ear-piercing cry, and I recognize Samson's lost raven, Inna. They must've sent her into the Shadows to call forth whatever is coming.

No sooner do I have that thought when large, spindly, black legs force their way through the opening, ripping apart this reality. More legs follow widening the entry to reveal a giant head. Eight shining, beady eyes cover the top portion and large pincers snap at the air beneath.

Squirming through the opening, is the biggest spider I have ever seen. With a wet, suction sound, the beast wriggles the rest of the way through. Riding atop, is another Reaper, but he is not like the others. Each hand has five long fingers tapered to points. His hood has been thrown back, showing off a creature from my nightmares.

A gaping mouth too large for its face is twisted into a mocking smile. The teeth within are pointed, each as long as one of my fingers. Sunken eyes glow red and stare out above hollow cheeks. There are no ears or nose and a shadow sits above his head, acting like hair, undulating on its own. The creature seems as large as a house, and Lyall move in to flank the large spider beast.

Shadows dance around the three large wolves, whose height only reach the middle of the spider's legs. I am outnumbered and absolutely terrified.

I wish Lucian were here.

"Welcome ta tha Three Kingdoms, Gabriel," Samson booms.

The creature's response echoes through my cerebellum. "Finally," he drawls, surveying the courtyard. Taking a deep breath, it continues, "Is this the girl you promised?" His red eyes land on me, freezing me in place.

"Yes, it is. She will open all tha doors we need," Samson moves to grab my shoulders, but I slice at his arms.

"You've found the other Seraphim Blade," he gasps, taking a few steps back in shock. I'm not sure why this surprises him but do not waste the opportunity to advance. Swinging at him with both arms, I back him toward the twins.

"Subdue her," the creature called Gabriel commands. The Lyall growl and begin to circle our small party.

The three traitors charge in a united front, and I slash at them all. My adrenaline kicks up, and the skin along my arms begins to tingle again. The hilts of the two blades I wield start to glow against my palms, the energy from my body feeding into the daggers. I wish I knew what was happening, but all I can do is continue to defend myself. My speed increases, and I am keeping pace with the twins, magic fueling my movements.

I land a blow on Aggie, slicing her cheek and Aric parries the blow from my right hand. I am possessed by a warrior spirit, the childhood training with my father has nothing on what I am capable of right now.

"Take the other dagger from her! The two together are formidable," Gabriel shouts.

This must be why my father took the other blade. I spin and block Samson's sword, not sure how much longer I can withstand their assault. I bring my hands too close together and the hilts of the daggers strike one another, the resulting blast sending all of us sprawling, and the Lyall scatter.

I've been thrown through the rift to the Shadows and land hard on the other side. I can see them all through the film in the barrier which is significantly smaller than it was before. Samson appears to be shouting something, charging toward the opening, but an idea comes to me before I can make out his words.

Slamming the hilts of the daggers together again, my reality disappears behind a muted mask. The opening has sewn itself back together. I am unscathed as I watch them all rebound of the resulting blow. Gabriel is unseated from the spider that has dug its legs into the dirt. I've cut off the connection.

Gabriel and his monsters cannot return. They cannot regenerate.

I have to get to the tower, I have to seal the other gateway. I may end up trapped, but that is what heroes do, right? Somehow, someway I will get to Glanchester and close the gateway there too. I will close them all if I can move through the Shadows undetected.

Again, I wish Lucian were here.

Luckily, the Shadow Territories reflect our own world, and I can navigate through the Keep relatively easy. It is though I am moving through a fog, elements are fuzzy and incorporeal, but I find the stairwell to the tower and start the ascent. Taking the stairs two at a time leaves me breathless.

I do not stop.

I think of Una and her children. Of my father, and all those who survived the massacre. I cannot let any more creatures through.

I make it to the top and see my world, vibrant in its simplicity through the other gateway. It is now or never. I bash the hilts together again and watch as the color dissipates. The two Reapers from earlier climb over the balcony wall and slam into an invisible barrier neither of us can see. I've done it, I've trapped them in that world. And I've trapped myself in this one.

I approach the Reapers, but they cannot see, nor touch me. It is as if I am a ghost. There is a looking glass by the balcony doors, and I catch my reflection, barely recognizing myself. My eyes are a glowing green, and my hair is unbound, floating around my shoulders like a soft breeze blows through the trees, but I feel nothing on my skin. For the first time in my life, I see beauty in my reflection, even in the muted colors of this reality and healing slash on my cheek.

What if Lucian saw me like this, I wonder?

Stepping out on the balcony, I watch the three turncoats scramble out of the courtyard. Gabriel is back atop his beast as it steps easily over the wall, with the Lyall racing ahead of them all. They head out of the city in the direction of Glanchester and an unaware group of survivors.

The trap door to the tunnels bursts open and smashes against the ground. Lucian, alive as ever, springs out of the opening with cuffs and chains attached to his wrists. They look similar to the set I saw in the torture chamber below. He lists to the side and falls to the ground.

I am so relieved that I shout his name, but he doesn't hear me. I try again and remember I am in the Shadows.

Racing back down to the courtyard I go to shake him but pass right through. I really am a ghost.

Thinking quickly, I slam the blades together again, but nothing happens. No rift. No ripple.

"Lucian!" I try again.

He gets to his feet and staggers toward the courtyard door, mumbling to himself, "Where are you Florence?"

His wrists look raw and seem to be smoking. Collapsing back to the ground his breathing is labored and gaze unfocused. He is lying parallel to my father and turns his head to take in his corpse. Closing his eyes, I see a tear fall from the corner of one.

He is dying.

"I'm too late," he says and tries again to stand but doesn't have the strength.

Tears of my own leak from my eyes, and I try to reach him through the veil. I attempt to recall the tingle from when I opened the gate before but, nothing comes.

I am numb.

The cold has wiped out all feeling, and my heart breaks all over again.

The Shadows have robbed me; I am surrounded by magic yet cannot reach to use it.

I focus on Lucian's face, trying to burn the lines of his perfect complexion into my memory. He didn't leave me, yet I cannot reach him. I may have saved myself, but I cannot save him.

This isn't how my story was supposed to go.

He expels a breath and doesn't take another.

His visage begins to waver, like it is trying to return to the atmosphere.

I fall to my knees next to him and scream into the void.

Chapter 21
Lucian

The ground above me thunders. The air has changed, charged with an electric current I recognize from the Shadows. What in the Three Kingdoms is happening? I hear Florence scream and never have I felt such urgency.

I must be close to the courtyard! That bitch doubled back and brought me to the basement of the Keep. I should've paid more attention, and I would've figured this out already. I can't beat myself up too much because I need to get to the surface.

I have no idea what is happening, but I know it cannot be good. I pull with all my might against the restraints and feel the wall behind me give.

My right arm comes flying outward, I've broken the links. Using that arm, I yank on the left chain, and it rips from the wall altogether. Now, to find a way out of this room.

Feeling my way along the walls I search for a catch, a pull, anything. I get to the opposite side of the cage and see a sconce set into the stone.

It's almost too obvious, but I try it anyway.

Pulling down on the light gives way to a door directly behind it. I am lethargic as strength leeches out of my body. I need to either get to Florence or the Shadows soon, or I will become a phantom. My limbs are starting to dissipate.

I burst into the main room of the basement and curse my stupidity all over again. The place where I was held must have been lined with Atrum too, muting my abilities. I was so close to Florence and didn't recognize it. There is no time to dwell as I stumble my way to the tunnels.

My breath is coming in short gasps, and I don't have a lot of time left. I was trying not to draw from Flor's energy too much, for fear she wouldn't accept this new fate. I am paying for it now.

Climbing the ladder to the trap door almost does me in, but thoughts of Florence in danger send me upward. I fling the door open and haul myself out. The air smells of decay and blood. The Reapers are here, and someone is dead.

I lie on the ground for a moment to gather my strength and hope that Florence is still alive.

A ripple in the air gets my attention but I don't see anything. I try to make it to the door in the courtyard, but I am too weak. I need dark magic. I need Florence.

"I'm too late," I say to the sky and imagine Flor there with me, soothing the ache in my limbs. I can feel myself letting go. The burden of being in the Shadows for years and the death of my cousin lifts from me as I picture her face, wishing I could see her one more time.

She is crying. Her eyes glowing like the grass after a rainstorm, vibrant and green. I don't want her to weep for me.

My body stills, all my muscles relaxing as one.

A weightlessness overtakes me, the breath escaping my lungs, never to return.

Epilogue
Lilyera

I flinch at the sound of Florence's devastated howl.

A brave girl who must do a brave thing.

My sanctuary is filled with the sounds of her pleading and the violins echo her lament.

She must lose herself among the wreckage and rise from the ashes of violence.

As it has been foretold.

Darkness moves in my oasis as I softly sing the hymns of my people.

A sad, haunting reverie of the reckoning.

We watched the violence scatter itself across the mines

Home they called through the sands

Demons marched in wretched lines

Devastating this holy land

Death is the creator of stories yet told

Bleeding out the plot

Come home sweet child, braving the cold

Wade through the rot

Tears fall down my cheeks and I know it has begun: The age of Darkness.

The age of Shadows.

I reach through the ether, speaking the languages of old, blessing our heroine.

Her eyes meet mine across space and time, cries becoming silent.

We are utterly still as the earth holds its breath.

Through the void I place a guiding hand.

"What has been set in motion cannot be undone. Fear cannot be outrun. You are the key, dear Florence. Find the blade lost to the Shadows. Find your center."

I sever the connection and fall back against the pillows, exhausted, awaiting the arrival of the council.

I have meddled where I should not have meddled and now must pay the price.

We must prepare for war.

Acknowledgments

This book started out as a silly project I never thought would actually see the light of day. I've been dreaming about becoming a published author since I was in fourth grade and being able to finally say I am is mind blowing. This is hopefully the beginning of something wonderful and I am excited to share it with you.

There are a few people I would like to give a special THANK YOU to:

Josh Moody, my husband and my cover artist. Thank you for constantly listening to me babble about this story and giving me the courage to let the world have it. You are my biggest supporter and have handled my mood-swings through this entire process gracefully. I am so grateful for you and the love we share.

AJ, my best friend, sounding board and fellow aspiring author. Thank you for being the first to read and critique this. You encouraged me to pursue my dreams and have been an incredible source of inspiration. You walked me through each existential crisis and breakthrough. I cannot wait to see what worlds you create. Cheers to traveling this path with me.

Courtney, my oldest and most cherished friend. We have been through hell and back together and I couldn't imagine life without you. You were my first fan and the only person who has read EVERYTHING I have ever written. Your constant support and light have shaped me into the writer I am. I cannot thank you enough for being with me through each stage of life and lifting me up when I needed it most. This book is for you.

Tifani, my friend, fellow YA lover and musician. Thank you for your instant and easy friendship and for letting me force this book on you from its inception. Your advice and encouragement have meant the absolute world to me. Having you back in my life has been a breath of fresh air and you aren't allowed to leave again :)

My parents. Thank you from the bottom of my heart for letting me be myself and for ALWAYS supporting whatever crazy dream I have. I owe everything I am to you both. You have helped me soar and have never stifled my creativity. Mom, thank you for being editor extrodinaire and giving this book a shot. I know it isn't your usual genre, but you helped make it amazing. You give me the confidence to be my own person and are always there to talk me off the ledge. I hope I am half the woman you are. Dad, thank you for always being my loudest and biggest supporter. No matter what decisions I make, you are always there to tell me I'm making you proud. You love this book more than anyone and that amazes me. I love you both. Thank you, endlessly.

Mary-Beth, my editor and friend. You might need the biggest thanks of them all. You've molded this mess into something acceptable and have made me confident in the fact that I have created something worth publishing. Knowing you love this and are ready for more is incredibly humbling. Your opinion was the scariest and most rewarding, so thank you. You are a badass and I'm so happy to have you in my corner. Thank you for everything.

Emma Hamm, new friend and amazing author. Thank you for taking the time to listen to me and guide a fledgling author through her first publication. Your advice and encouraging words helped get this project off the ground. Thank you for your stories and your support, it means so much.

And finally, everyone who has asked about the book and told me they couldn't wait to read it. That alone is amazing to me and I can't believe so many friends are supportive of this new, scary chapter in my life. Thank you, thank you, thank you. I hope you loved it and are ready for the next installment.

21968459R00102

Made in the USA
Columbia, SC
22 July 2018